I'LL BE HOME FOR CHRISTMAS

A SADDLE HILL CHRISTMAS MYSTERY

ERIN LANTER

For Zoe, the biggest elf I know.

I'LL BE HOME FOR CHRISTMAS

CHAPTER ONE

December 21st

A LIGHT SNOW fell on Saddle Hill, Kentucky as Bing Crosby crooned "White Christmas" in the background. Marian Bright put the finishing touches on the hot cocoa bar she'd set up for the volunteer choir to enjoy after their first annual Christmas caroling outing.

Last Christmas, the whole community banded together when a jewelry theft rocked the town. This year, the town council decided to celebrate the first official day of winter by making Christmas caroling on the winter solstice an annual event.

Marian took a step back to scrutinize the buffet. Homemade hot chocolate mix, mini marshmallows, whipped cream, sprinkles, and even crushed candy canes promised to bring warmth and comfort to the carolers after standing outside in the frigid night air.

"Perfect," she muttered with a satisfied smile on her face. Dressed in one of her many Christmas sweaters—this one with a Christmas tree complete with colorful puff-ball ornaments sewn onto the knit boughs—seventy-three-year-old Marian was delighted to bring Christmas cheer to everyone, young and old, on this beautiful evening.

"I'm ready to go whenever you are," Holly Berry announced, emerging from her bedroom.

Marian, the joy of the season etched on her face, turned to study the young woman walking toward her. Holly, who'd come to stay with her for the Christmas season last year, had never left. With a troubled past and a police record, Holly had been more than willing to start a new life in Saddle Hill. As a recent widow, Marian had been happy to have Holly move in with her.

"That looks wonderful!" Holly exclaimed, admiring the hot cocoa bar Marian had so lovingly arranged.

Turning her attention back to the buffet, she said, "Thank you, dear. I'm afraid it's not complete without Nadine's Christmas cookies, though."

"Is she still bringing them?" Holly asked as she adjusted her scarf and flipped her long red hair over her shoulder.

"Yes. I talked to her about an hour ago, and she's feeling well enough to come caroling with us, too. It will be such a wonderful evening." Marian turned back toward Holly.

What a lovely young woman, she thought. At twenty-six years old, Holly finally seemed happy. No thanks to her parents who criticized everything she did and were incapable of being civil to each other, Marian mused.

"Do I look okay?" Holly asked and turned in a circle, her voice betraying her nervousness about the evening. With her slender figure and shimmering hair, she'd caught the eye of many young men in town. The only one she was interested in, though, was Eli Nolan, a sheriff's deputy she'd met last year when she'd been locked in a storage closet by her boss's ex-wife.

With all the tenderness of a doting grandmother, Marian said, "You look wonderful, dear. Eli won't be able to keep his eyes off you."

Holly blushed and fiddled with the scarf. "Thank you for this scarf. It's beautiful."

"It should keep that pretty little neck of yours warm tonight. Much better than that ratty old thing you had been wearing," Marian said. "Let me get my jacket, and we'll be on our way."

As she retrieved her fur-lined jacket and slid it on over her Christmas sweater, Marian thought, with as peaceful as things are this year, this might just be the best Christmas yet.

CHAPTER TWO

"ARE YOU ALMOST ready, Joe?" Nadine called as she slid the last of the Christmas cookies onto the platter. "We need to meet the other carolers at the community center in fifteen minutes."

"Just a minute," Joe replied. He settled into his favorite chair to tie his snow boots, then stood and shook his pant legs down to his ankles. "Ready," he announced, then walked into the kitchen where his wife was putting the finishing touches on the plate of Christmas cookies.

"What do you think?" Nadine asked, looking up into Joe's eyes.

"I think you're the most beautiful woman I've ever laid eyes on," he said, and gently kissed her forehead.

The corner of Nadine's mouth drooped. "I mean about the cookies. Does this look okay?"

Joe shifted his eyes to the confections in assorted Christmas shapes. "Wonderful, as always. But, you know, you don't always have to garnish your platters of cookies. This is just for the volunteer carolers," he teased.

Nadine's doe-brown eyes narrowed. "So what? I want it to look good, no matter who it's for."

He wrapped his arms around her. "Your pastries aren't good because of the way they look, although they are beautiful. They're good because you love the people you make them for."

She smiled and rested her head on his shoulder. "This *will* be a great evening, won't it?"

"Mmmm-hmmm," Joe agreed. A concerned look flitted across his face. "You sure you're up to this? I mean, that's a long time to be standing in the cold. I just don't want anything to happen…"

"I'm fine, really. I admit this has been a hard year for me—for both of us—with the miscarriage and all, but this little guy is strong. The way he pummels me, he certainly won't let me forget that." Nadine placed her hands on her basketball-shaped stomach. "I bet he'll love hearing the songs we sing."

Joe hesitated. "If you're sure."

"I am." Standing straighter, she said, "Now, will you please cover that platter with plastic wrap while I try to get my boots on. Before long, I'm going to need you to help me."

He watched as she walked to the coat closet to retrieve her snow boots. What a year it had been. After getting married last Christmas Eve, it had been a whirlwind of life changes. Shortly after the new year, Sheriff Arnold left Saddle Hill in search of another position in a bigger city, and Joe had been elected as the new sheriff. With years of experience as mall security under his belt, he helped catch the thief who'd stolen a special Christmas piece from the local jewelry store, Stockton's Jewel Palace, last year.

If that wasn't a big enough change, Wanda Kirk, the owner of the Rose Petal Café where Nadine was the pastry chef, abruptly decided to retire, giving Nadine the opportunity to buy the small restaurant. After weeks of going back and forth about whether or not she wanted the responsibility, Nadine decided that she'd love to have her own place. For the past several months, she'd been working long hours putting her own personal touch on the café. The result was a warm and welcoming environment staffed by smiling employees who went out of their way to make the customers feel welcome.

Somewhere in the middle of that transition, they'd found out Nadine was pregnant. A few months later, they'd been devastated by her miscarriage late in the first trimester. With this second pregnancy, Joe found it impossible not to treat Nadine like she'd break every time the wind blew. He knew Nadine was aware of what he was doing, but as patient as she was, she never let him see her frustration.

Now, as he watched her struggle to lace up her snow boots, he was overwhelmed by the knowledge that there was no one else he'd rather go through the whirlwind with.

Nadine sighed, pulling Joe from his revelry. As she stood, she said, "You might have to help me with my shoes sooner than I thought."

Joe turned his attention to her feet, where the laces on her boots were a jumbled mess of knots. He bent over to fix them. "We can't have you tripping on these when they come untied."

"Thanks," Nadine said as she wrapped a scarf around her neck and pulled on a warm hat to cover her light brown hair, then pulled on her brown, puffy jacket. "I look like a burnt marshmallow," she said wryly, but forced a smile. "Let's go bring Christmas cheer to the masses."

Balancing the platter of cookies on one hand and tucking the other under Nadine's elbow to steady her on the snowy steps, Joe relished the upcoming serenity of the next several days. As long as everything went as planned, he and Nadine would celebrate their last Christmas with just the two of them in perfect peace.

CHAPTER THREE

"BUT WHY CAN'T I wear my Santa suit?" James Jingle complained to his wife, Patricia, as they bundled up for the town's first annual Christmas caroling event.

Patricia rolled her eyes. "Because we're going to sing to people as *neighbors*, not the Clauses," she explained.

"It's just a few days until Christmas, though. Don't you think that's an acceptable time to be Santa?" he argued.

Patricia shot James a warning look as she put the finishing touches on her hair, which she'd recently had cut into a fashionable, chin-length bob.

For decades, she'd worn her hair in a bun, just as Mrs. Claus would. After giving James an ultimatum about all the problems their year-round Christmas caused, she'd shown him the manuscript of the memoir she'd been working on. *Forever Mrs. Claus* came out last week, and tomorrow she'd be doing her first book signing at Dusty Jackets, the local bookstore.

Over the past year, she'd spread her wings in the fashion department, and no longer wore only red, white, and green. Her hair had been the final change.

Her husband, James, the patriarch of the Jingle family, hadn't been so eager to make the change. He still looked uncomfortable in anything other than Santa-approved apparel, though he did recognize the need to move on from the traditions that had created a wedge between their oldest son, Kris, and the rest of the family.

As James shifted the suspenders that were holding up the now-too-baggy jeans, Patricia looked at him with compassion. He really was trying to live like a regular person, though regular wasn't something that came naturally to him.

She'd cut the amount of Christmas sweets he'd been allowed to eat throughout the year, which accounted for the pants that no longer fit and his lower blood sugar and cholesterol levels. As a treat for his hard work and *mostly* positive attitude, Patricia retrieved a Christmas cookie from the stash she kept hidden in the back of the freezer. Deciding that he deserved the biggest one, she popped it in the microwave for several seconds, then put it on their most festive plate, and carried it back to their bedroom where James was buttoning a red-plaid, flannel shirt over his suspenders.

Scowling as he buttoned, he said, "Do you think this should be tucked in? I don't know how to do that with suspenders on."

She smiled at her husband of more than forty years, held the plate out toward him, and was rewarded with the jolly smile she hadn't seen lately.

"It might help if you wore the suspenders *over* your shirt. Then you'd be able to tuck it in," Patricia suggested.

Eyes focused only on the plate she was holding, he said, "Really? That's a big one!" His face glowed like a child's as he snatched the cookie off the plate and took a large bite.

"Yes, but hurry up. We need to get to the community center to meet everyone. I don't want to miss the first year of town-wide Christmas caroling."

Crumbs fell onto James's shirt as he ate the cookie. "I'm hurrying," he mumbled, dropping more crumbs out of his mouth. He dropped the suspenders off his shoulders and put the shirt back on. He stuffed it into the waist of his jeans, and pulled the suspenders back up. "Oh, this does help," he muttered.

"I'm really excited about tonight," Patricia said as she brushed a wrinkle out of her sweater. "This will be such a good way to kick off the official winter season, and it could be the last time we see some of our friends before Christmas Day. Then we'll go back to Marian's house to visit with everyone and warm up. She brags about her top-secret hot chocolate recipe, so I can't wait to try it."

"All her recipes are top secret," James said as they walked out of the bedroom and down the stairs to the living room, where the lights on the Christmas tree winked at them. "I hate to admit it, but Christmas does feel more magical when we don't have the tree up all the time. I guess I didn't realize that I'd gotten so used to seeing it that I didn't really even notice it anymore."

"I know more than you give me credit for," Patricia teased. "Now, put on your shoes and coat. We've got to get going or we'll be late."

James settled onto the sofa and pulled on his fleece-lined snow boots, then stood and wrapped the hand-knit scarf Patricia made for him several years ago around his neck, donned his earmuffs, and stuffed his hands into his gloves. "Ready," he announced.

"Good. Let's go."

As they drove toward the community center, Christmas music filled the car and the joy of the season was written on both their faces.

"Do you think Kris will be there tonight?" James asked, a hopeful note in his voice. He'd been working hard the last year to mend the broken relationship with his oldest son, though sometimes he felt like he was trying too hard.

"I don't know. He might be busy with that new girlfriend of his," Patricia said. "I'm glad he seems happy, though. It's been a long time since he's been happy."

James nodded in agreement. "Too bad Nicholas won't be able to be there."

Patricia didn't answer. Instead, she looked out the window, watching the snow fall.

Nicholas wouldn't be eligible for parole for another year.

She sighed. There's no way this Christmas could be harder than last year, she mused. With the exception of her youngest son sitting in jail for robbing Stockton's Jewel Palace last year and framing his older brother, everything this year was picture-perfect.

Leaning her head back on the headrest, she closed her eyes and smiled. This promised to be a very merry Christmas, indeed, and tonight was just what the town needed.

Looking out at the gentle snowfall, Patricia believed nothing could possibly ruin this perfect night.

CHAPTER FOUR

RALPH STOCKTON BEAMED at his new bride as she pulled on her snow boots.

After a disastrous two-year marriage to Brenda Morris, he'd had the marriage annulled when she was caught sabotaging the jewelry in his store and stealing a diamond tennis bracelet worth several thousand dollars.

Once the hurt and anger wore off, he'd felt like a fool for thinking someone like Brenda would ever be interested in him without an ulterior motive. It had been a whirlwind romance, the aftermath leaving him reeling with regret.

Now, only a year after the annulment, he was married to the love of his life, Carla Whipple. It had also been Carla who always understood him, and it was Carla who shared his love for small-town living. It had been Carla whose heart he'd broken when he met and married Brenda.

Unfortunately, it had also been Carla who, saying she missed him and thought the star represented the very best of him, broke into Ralph's safe at Stockton's Jewel Palace last year and stole one of the prototypes for the Christmas piece he'd designed in an effort to save his store. He couldn't bring himself to press charges against someone he cared so deeply about, so they rekindled their romance instead.

Carla had even managed to get Ralph to do something he never thought he would: he sold his childhood home where he'd lived his whole life and moved into a house where he and Carla could start over. Carla had said, and Ralph agreed, that they wanted to live somewhere "that wretched Brenda had never set foot in." This house even had a garage, a feature Ralph never thought was necessary and Brenda always pointed out made the house no better than a shack. Now that it was winter, he had to agree that it was nice not having to scrape the car every time it snowed.

"Ready," Carla announced, as she pulled down her toboggan hat far enough to cover her ears and forehead.

"Me, too," Ralph agreed once he'd torn his admiring gaze away from his wife. "Let's go."

As they pulled out of the garage of the brand-new house, Andy Williams sang "It's the Most Wonderful Time of the Year" on the car radio.

Thoughtful silence drifted between the newlyweds as they each reflected on how different their lives were this Christmas compared to last.

"Can you believe how much has changed in the past year?" Carla asked, gazing lovingly at her new husband. "I never thought I'd be married to the man of my dreams by Christmas."

Ralph returned her gaze briefly before turning his attention back to the road. "And after being married to Brenda, I never thought I'd be happy again."

Carla could see his eyes sparkling with mischief. "I can't

imagine the queen being willing to stand outside in the snow, singing to people she hates… which was everybody."

Ralph chuckled warmly. "Unfortunately that's true. Her royal highness would think a warm jacket would make her look fat. Not to mention the unflattering way the cold would turn her nose red."

"Hail to the queen," they said in unison, then burst into laughter.

Ralph reached across the center console and grasped Carla's gloved hand. He raised it to his mouth and kissed her fingers. His life was so different than it had been just a year ago. A new business opportunity had taken care of all his financial worries that had nearly cost him his store last year, and Carla had come back into his life, providing love and companionship when he was certain he'd be trapped in a loveless marriage forever, facing a lifetime of loneliness.

Ralph smiled again, this time at his good fortune. It truly was the most wonderful time of the year, and, remembering how the town had come together to help him last year, Ralph could hardly wait to spread the joy he felt with everyone else.

CHAPTER FIVE

SYLVIA BELL DROPPED her bag on the entry table and sighed. It would be so nice to spend Christmas in Saddle Hill. Far from the hustle and bustle of the city, she planned to spend the next five days relaxing in the comfort of her country cottage.

A designer from New York, Sylvia had been desperate to get away from it all last year and stumbled upon the Mountain Craft Festival in Saddle Hill, Kentucky. Instantly falling in love with the slower pace and hometown feel, she became even more enamored when she met Ralph Stockton, a talented jeweler who was showcasing a new piece for the Christmas season. She was impressed by his attention to detail and the care he put into his work and knew immediately she wanted him to be head of design for the new jewelry line for her brand, Jersey Belle.

A year later, his pieces were wildly successful, and they'd settled into an easy partnership and solid friendship.

Sylvia couldn't help but wonder, though, how it might have turned out if Ralph was still married to her college roommate, Brenda Morris. The only hesitation she'd had about working with Ralph was the fact that he'd married such a cruel, materialistic woman.

To her relief, that ship had sailed. Ralph made tons of money, and Brenda hadn't been able to touch a dime of it.

In a great twist of irony, Ralph even sold his childhood home, which he'd insisted that he'd never do. Once he rekindled his relationship with Carla Whipple, he insisted they needed a fresh start, and was more than happy to settle into a house that Brenda Morris-Stockton had never set foot in. The bullied, chubby girl Sylvia had once been—the one that still lived inside her—loved that Ralph was doing the things Brenda had wanted him to do, and she wouldn't be able to enjoy a bit of it.

Inhaling deeply, she relished the calming scent of cedar and lavender that always welcomed her back. More and more, Saddle Hill felt like home.

She loved New York. The excitement of living there was in her blood. Lately, though, she'd wondered if maybe there wasn't more to life than moving from one work commitment to the next, spending nearly all her waking hours at the mercy of the fickle tastes of the consumer.

With increasing frequency, Sylvia realized she didn't have anyone she could really talk to. Sure, she had colleagues, but the relationships with them were superficial at best. There was no one in the city she could think of that was a true friend. She'd tried talking to her mom about her growing discontentment, but her mother had waved it off saying Sylvia was just having an early midlife crisis.

"After all," her mom had said many times, "you have everything you'd ever dreamed. How can you possibly be unhappy?"

It was true, Sylvia's career was everything she'd ever

dreamed. Her personal life, however, she described as a gaping abyss of loneliness.

Her mom had just rolled her eyes and told her to stop being so dramatic.

But here in Saddle Hill, Sylvia had everything she felt like her life was missing. Everyone had welcomed her so warmly, she never once felt like an outsider. She had friends here. A family.

Sylvia took another deep breath, inhaling the earthy fragrance of her cottage, turned the heat up to a toasty seventy-four degrees, then moved quickly from room to room, making sure everything was in order. Noting that the place was ship-shape, she quickly changed into fleece-lined jeans, snow boots, and a parka. It was the town's first annual Christmas caroling event, and she was determined to be there.

Glancing at the clock, she realized the vans would be pulling out of the community center parking lot soon. She grabbed her keys and her tote, then dashed back to her still-warm car.

She turned up her Kenny G Christmas album, then backed her car out of the driveway. Christmas vacation was starting off just right, and she wouldn't let anything spoil the feeling she had of being completely at home in Saddle Hill.

CHAPTER SIX

EXCITED MURMURS FILLED the Saddle Hill Community
Center as the carolers gathered in small groups, anticipating
their first stop. Bundled in their warmest winter attire, the
townspeople were filled with happy anticipation.

Marian looked around at the neighbors, friends, and
friends-turned-family who had gathered, pride swelling in her
chest. Since her late husband, Roger, passed away eighteen
months ago, she'd relied on the townspeople to be her family.

They certainly had become that.

She smiled as she watched pink creep up Holly's neck and
fill her cheeks at something Eli Nolan, Holly's first love interest
since moving to Saddle Hill last Christmas, had said. He was
a nice young man, and Marian approved of their budding
romance. It didn't hurt that his whole job was about obeying
the letter of the law. That would keep him out of trouble and
Holly from going off track. Without any grandchildren of her
own, Marian had come to love Holly like a granddaughter, and
occasionally worried that Holly's troubled past would catch

up to her. Other than some suspicion for theft last Christmas, Holly had kept her nose clean and lived above reproach.

Sylvia Bell, looking like she just stepped off the cover of a magazine despite being bundled for the cold, was huddled in a small group with Ralph and Carla, Joe and Nadine, and Patricia and James Jingle. Nadine Adler looked radiant and only slightly uncomfortable as she rubbed circles on her belly. Joe stood very close to her, almost as though he was trying to protect her from anything that might harm her or the little one she carried. Newlyweds Ralph and Carla stood with their arms around each other, smiling into one another's eyes every minute or so. Marian stifled a chuckle as she watched James tug on his clothing. He was still uncomfortable dressed in anything other than Santa-approved apparel, even though he'd had the past year to practice wearing normal clothes.

Along with Holly, these were the people she loved most.

Taking strides as long as her five-foot two-inch frame could handle, Marian crossed the room to her friends. Sylvia greeted Marian with a hug, her willowy height dwarfing the older woman.

"It's so good to see you," Sylvia said, tightening the hug. "Being here with you all feels like coming home."

Marian grabbed Sylvia's hand and gave it a squeeze. Her eyes twinkled as she said, "Maybe you should be here more often."

"That's what we were just telling her," Ralph interjected, his gaze once again falling on his new bride. "It's just not the same when she's not here."

"I get away from New York as often as I can…" Sylvia's tone was wistful. "I have obligations there."

Eager chatter surrounded Marian in all directions. She

couldn't be happier that her fellow townspeople would be coming back to her house for refreshments after they were finished caroling.

A loud clap interrupted the conversations, and a hush fell over the group when Becky Roswell, Saddle Hill's mayor, cleared her throat and continued to clap her hands together.

Her blue eyes sparkled as she addressed the crowd. "Thank you all for joining in on this spectacularly festive occasion. You are what make this town so special," she gushed. "I have the pleasure to introduce you all to Carol Ling, a reporter with WGNN, *We're the Good News Network*. It's a privilege to have Carol with us, documenting our town's Christmas traditions, leading off with our first annual Christmas caroling event. Let's give Ms. Ling our warmest Saddle Hill welcome." The mayor paused to allow the applause and hum of excitement to quiet down. "Please split up into groups of ten and make your way to the vans we have waiting to drive you to the stops. And don't forget to enter the contest to name our newly established winter solstice Christmas caroling. You can drop your entry into the box over there." She waved toward the back corner of the atrium of the community center. "The winner will receive a tray of baked goods from the Rose Petal Café, courtesy of our very own Nadine Adler."

The mayor led the group in appreciative applause, her dark blond hair bouncing with the effort, then turned on her heel and stepped out from the middle of the crowd, shaking a few hands on her way to one of the vans. The reporter walked beside her, glancing toward different groups as they all filed toward the vans. She smiled and ducked her head as she climbed into the passenger side of the mayor's van.

"Okay! Let's get this show on the road!" James Jingle cried above the other voices. "Let's go spread some Christmas cheer!"

Whoops went up from the carolers, and they all moved toward the vans that were chartered for the occasion. Piling into the vans, happily chattering to one another, no observer would believe anything sinister could ever happen in this idyllic little town.

CHAPTER SEVEN

AT THE FIRST stop, the carolers hurried from the vans and lined up in the yard of the initial recipient of their Christmas cheer.

As the carolers' voices rang out in perfect harmony, a sideways glance at Holly revealed that she and Eli Nolan were holding hands in the center of the group, clearly more interested in each other than in serenading the town. Marian smiled. The girl certainly could use a little happiness in her life.

Joe Adler's arm was draped protectively around Nadine's lower back as her sweet soprano voice led the chorus of "Silent Night."

Ralph and Carla Stockton were huddled close together, their voices blending as well as their rekindled romance had over the past year.

Sylvia Bell stood near the Stocktons, snowflakes getting caught in the dark waves of her hair. She looked happy, like she was home.

The other faces of Saddle Hill residents shone with a joy Marian would never tire of seeing. The ache of losing Roger had lessened in the past year, and she credited her friends who'd become her family. They'd kept her going on the occasions when the loneliness felt that it would consume her, and in the rare instances when she felt all alone in the world, they reminded her that she belonged with them.

How could anyone get by without friends like these? she wondered as warmth spread through her chest and midsection, making the otherwise blustery winter evening feel like a mild March day.

What better way to show our appreciation for this special town than to delight the townspeople with familiar and comforting carols? Marian was sure Saddle Hill would be a better place because of the way they'd pulled together to bring cheer.

House after house offered an opportunity for the carolers to show what a beautiful occasion the winter solstice could be. Despite the below-freezing temperatures that were responsible for making eyes water, noses run, and toes go numb, the spirit of goodwill hadn't dampened a bit. Chattering from excitement and as an effort to warm up their faces, the conversation inside the vans was both jolly and hopeful.

At the last house, they all agreed to make this the best performance yet. With Marian on handbells and James Jingle on harmonica, the group crooned "There's No Christmas Like a Home Christmas." Marian was certain Perry Como himself couldn't have done a better job.

As the choir launched into the first stanza of "We Wish You a Merry Christmas," the front door opened and a gruff-looking man in his mid-sixties stepped out onto the porch. With renewed excitement, the carolers raised their voices even louder. With a live audience, they were out to impress.

As they sang their hearts out, the man yelled, "Quiet! Get off my property!"

The bells stopped ringing, the harmonica stopped playing, and the carolers shared confused glances with one another as the singing died off. The man wore faded flannel pajama bottoms, a dingy white tee shirt with a hole under one armpit, and fuzzy bedroom slippers as he descended the steps onto his front walk.

Looking for all the world like he was intent on raising a ruckus, the choir moved back a few feet, Joe's arm tightening around Nadine and Eli's hand squeezing Holly's hand before he dropped it and moved toward the front of the group.

"Hello, Mr. Feinstein," the young deputy said, moving slowly toward the man. "It's a lovely night, isn't it?"

"It was until you all started bellowing out here on my front lawn. I want you to leave," he demanded.

Marian stepped toward the front of the group and sidled up next to Eli. "Good evening, Henry. How are you doing?"

"Terrible. I have a splitting headache, and here you are clanging those bells and howling outside my house," he grumbled. "You sound like a pack of dogs."

Marian turned on her brightest smile, the one she typically saved for the children who came to sit on Santa's lap at the mall. A mall elf for seventeen years and running, there hadn't been a single crying child she hadn't been able to cheer up, and she was confident she could do the same for Henry Feinstein.

"Now, Mr. Feinstein. This is the most wonderful time of the year. There's no need to come out here yelling at us this way," she gently scolded, still holding her smile in place.

Henry Feinstein took several steps forward and stopped just in front of Marian. Snow crept up the sides of his slippers and threatened to slide down into them as he stood toe to toe with Saddle Hill's merriest elf. "Get off my property," he growled.

Marian could smell the whiskey on his breath and feared he was falling back into the drinking problem that had gotten him in trouble for breaking and entering and assault several years back.

Eli slipped his hand under Marian's elbow and gently guided her toward the vans where the other carolers were boarding. She shook it off and walked back to the grumpy man.

"Merry Christmas, Mr. Feinstein," she said, then turned to leave.

"I hate Christmas, and I hate you! You'll be sorry you bothered me," Henry slurred, whatever he'd been drinking clearly having an effect on him.

Marian shook her head and turned back toward the vans that would take them all back to the community center. Clearly there was somebody in Saddle Hill she couldn't consider a friend. A slight chill that had nothing to do with the cold raced down Marian's spine.

Marian knew his story and could understand how losing a spouse could breed anger and resentment, as well as a feeling of hopelessness. If it hadn't been for her friends and her natural cheery disposition, she might have been tempted to go down the same path.

There had to be something she could do to bring some cheer to the man. As she buckled her seatbelt, a plan formed in her mind. She would extend friendship to Henry Feinstein even if he didn't want it. Everybody needed a friend, especially at Christmas.

Besides, she assured herself, that wasn't really a threat. *Telling me I'd be sorry I bothered him was just the ranting of a drunk and lonely man. Surely, he wouldn't actually do anything to hurt me.*

CHAPTER EIGHT

MARIAN SAT QUIETLY in the back of the van on the way back to the Saddle Hill Community Center. Everyone around her spoke enthusiastically about the night and voiced their dismay at the way Henry Feinstein had behaved when all they were trying to do was spread a little Christmas cheer. A few of the carolers murmured defenses or explanations about his harsh words and confrontational manner.

"He'd been drinking…"

"You know he hasn't been right since his wife died…"

"Being in jail changed him…"

"He's not really one of us, you know. He wasn't born here…"

"Of course he didn't want to have us sing Christmas carols. Isn't he Jewish? We should have known better."

Marian listened to each of the reasons why the others thought Henry hadn't been welcoming of the carolers who serenaded him and thought that while all those things might have contributed to his gruff demeanor, something else was probably going on. A man doesn't just self-destruct that way without a reason.

"You're awfully quiet," Holly leaned over and whispered in Marian's ear.

Forcing a smile, Marian nodded. "Sorry, dear. Just lost in thought. Did you have fun?"

Holly blushed and her eyes shifted toward Eli, who was resting his head against the seat with his eyes closed. "It was a lot of fun."

Marian's smile was genuine this time. "Eli is one lucky fellow to have caught your eye."

Her blush deepening to darker red, Holly thanked Marian and looped her arm through the older woman's. "I can tell something is bothering you. What's going on?"

"I remember when Henry Feinstein's wife died," Marian said with a sigh. "Roger and I were friendly with the Feinsteins and would sometimes get together for dinner and a game of bridge. After she died, he was a broken shell of a man, and even though there were times when it seemed like he'd lost all reason for living, I never knew him to be confrontational the way he was tonight."

"I didn't know you knew him," Holly remarked. "I've never even heard you mention him."

A wave of guilt washed over Marian. It was true. She hadn't kept up with him the last year and a half the way she should have. She gulped and nodded. "Roger kept their friendship going after Henry's wife died, but I didn't think it was appropriate for me to be going around with a recent widower. When Roger died, I didn't even think to check on Henry to see how he was doing. Roger was a good friend to him, and I'm sure he was grieving."

"I guess that would explain why he wasn't too happy when you started talking to him tonight," Holly observed, casting a sideways glance toward Eli, who seemed to have drifted to sleep.

A nod was Marian's only answer. "Is Joe working Eli too hard?" Marian asked, tilting her head in Eli's direction.

"No. Joe is a hard worker and that has really taken a lot of stress off Eli. He actually has less work than when Sheriff Arnold was running the show. Anything he didn't want to do, he always passed on to Eli." A sly smile curved Holly's lips. "We've been up late talking most nights. I really, really like him."

Marian's smile matched Holly's. Her eyes twinkled. "I can tell."

"I really hope things work out with him," she whispered close to Marian's ear, obviously trying to make sure Eli didn't overhear just how smitten she was.

"I know," Marian said, patting the young woman's hand.

As the van pulled into the parking lot of the community center and the carolers disembarked, Marian caught Holly's shoulder. "Would you mind having Eli take you home? I've got to run an errand really quick. It shouldn't take long, so go ahead and get the party started without me."

Holly's mouth drooped. "But this whole shindig was your idea, and it's your famous hot chocolate," she protested.

Suddenly distracted, Marian shook her head, patted Holly's hand, and mumbled, "It'll be fine." She walked toward her car, leaving Holly to wonder what had gotten into the woman who'd become like a grandmother to her.

෴

Back at Marian's house, the carolers broke into song as they drank steaming mugs of hot cocoa, eggnog that was probably spiked, and nibbled on Nadine's assortment of Christmas cookies. It was a merry occasion, and nearly everyone was in good spirits.

Everyone except Holly.

She wrung her hands, an unconscious gesture she'd picked up from Marian.

Where could she be? Holly wondered.

It had been almost two hours since the crowd arrived at their house, and Marian was nowhere to be seen.

"What's got you so worried?" a masculine voice said from behind her.

Holly smiled despite her mounting anxiety, then sobered immediately. "Marian hasn't gotten here yet. Something is wrong, I can feel it. She'd never miss this party. Look at all the work she put into getting ready for it." Holly waved her hand toward the buffet table.

Eli's eyebrows bunched together. "You said she was acting funny. Did she give you any indication where she might have been going?"

Shaking her head, Holly felt herself frowning. "None. She just said she had an errand to run." Holly's voice sounded hoarse even to her own ears, as though the tension she felt had crept into her throat.

Eli chewed his bottom lip, a mannerism Holly had learned meant he was thinking. Finally, he said, "I'll tell you what. Why don't I go out and drive around a bit and see if I can find her? I'm sure she's fine, but just in case the roads have gotten slick, I'll have a look around for her. Her car probably just slid off the road or something."

Holly's stomach dropped as she considered the possibility of Marian having been in an accident. She hoped that wasn't the case, but also realized that sliding off the road was preferable to what she was becoming afraid had happened. Marian had a cell phone, and if she'd been able to use it, she would have.

As Holly watched, Eli crossed the room and whispered something in Joe Adler's ear, then walked out the front door and into the snowy night. The feeling that there hadn't been an accident gnawed at her, and Holly couldn't shake the feeling that Eli wouldn't find anything.

Her gut told her Marian's car hadn't slid off the road. It told her that whatever happened to Marian was much, much worse.

CHAPTER NINE

"WHAT HAPPENED WITH Eli?" Nadine asked as she snuggled close to Joe in bed. Though she'd been out of the freezing air for hours, she still couldn't seem to warm up. A slight shiver raced down her spine, and she did her best to hide it from Joe. The last thing he needed was to worry about whether or not she was okay after caroling, especially since he didn't think she should have gone in the first place.

Joe pulled the covers up to his chin and slid his hand over to rest on Nadine's growing belly. "Marian didn't come to the party, and Holly was nervous. Eli went to check it out. He thought maybe Marian's car slid off the road or something."

Nadine propped herself up on one elbow, her pretty doe-brown eyes filled with worry. "That's true. I was getting so tired that I didn't notice who was or wasn't there. Why wouldn't Marian come to the party she was hosting?"

Propping himself up to come to eye-level with Nadine, Joe brushed her hair out of her face and tucked it behind her ear. "You were tired? Are you okay?"

Mentally chastising herself for mentioning her fatigue, she smiled. "Yes, of course. It's just exhausting to grow this little guy."

"If you're sure…"

"I am," Nadine said firmly. "Did Eli find her?"

Joe settled back onto his pillow and slunk farther down under the covers. "I don't know. Haven't heard."

Nadine frowned at her husband. She loved him, but he could be so dense sometimes. "Well, can you ask him? Marian is our friend, and I'm worried."

"Oh, yeah. I guess I should," Joe muttered as if he hadn't considered it before. He reached over and grabbed his phone from the nightstand. He tapped the screen several times, then set it down on the covers next to his hip. "If Eli is still awake, he'll probably get back to me soon."

Nadine sighed and lowered herself back to her pillow, then rolled onto her side. She wedged an extra pillow under her stomach for support. "I feel so guilty. How could I not have noticed that Marian wasn't at the party? I should have sensed that something was wrong. I'm sure Holly is worried sick, and I haven't done a thing to help her."

"Don't be so hard on yourself, Nay. It's not your responsibility to make sure everyone is okay."

Nadine sighed. Joe was right, of course. It was something she knew she needed to work on, especially before the baby came. Once she had a baby to take care of, there would be less of her to go around.

Joe's phone pinged, indicating he'd received a text.

Sitting up as quickly as she could, Nadine scooted closer in an effort to see the screen. When she couldn't, she asked, "What did he say?"

The way Joe's mouth drooped at the corners told her that whatever news Eli had shared wasn't good. He turned the screen where Nadine could read it, and her heart sank.

No sign of her.

"You mean he didn't see her or her car out *anywhere*?" Nadine pressed. "How could that be possible? She has to be somewhere. Holly must be absolutely beside herself."

She grabbed her own phone and pulled up Holly's information. Quickly tapping out a text, she pressed send and held her breath. Surely the reason Eli hadn't found Marian's car was because she'd already parked it in her own driveway and was tucked snugly in her flannel sheets.

She's not home yet, Holly had replied. *I don't know what to do. Eli said he saw her car parked near that Feinstein man's house, but that there was no sign of her.*

Nadine groaned and sent a reply to Holly.

I'm on my way.

As she climbed out of bed and headed to the closet, Joe said, "Hey, where are you going?"

"Over to Holly's. She needs a friend right now, and as long as I'm still able to be there for her, I'm going to be."

Joe huffed but said nothing. It would be useless to argue. Nadine wasn't one to let anyone stand in the way when she thought she should be there for a friend.

After a quick "I love you" and a kiss on Joe's forehead, Nadine disappeared from the bedroom. "Make sure you let me know if you hear anything," she called to him just before she opened the door to the garage and started the engine of her car.

"Sure thing," he muttered, silently praying she'd be safe on the road tonight and that there wouldn't be a danger to Nadine or the baby. He also couldn't help but be afraid that if another person was responsible for whatever had happened to Marian, a pregnant woman out and about at night by herself would be at risk of sharing the same fate.

CHAPTER TEN

December 22

THE NEXT MORNING at the Saddle Hill Mall, a group of mall employees huddled together whispering as they waited for Winston Marshall, the mall manager, to take his place on the stage of "Santa's Workshop."

Ready to begin the countdown of the last few days of the Christmas shopping season, they all knew Winston would expect them to be at their cheerful best to make as many sales as possible.

Ralph and Carla Stockton were sitting close together, each looking like they were ready to get to their own businesses, Stockton's Jewel Palace and Carla's candle shop, Whipple's Wicks. Ralph's financial windfall after partnering with Sylvia Bell's *Jersey Belle* clothing line had provided the income they needed to save their stores, which had both been in danger of shutting their doors forever only a year ago.

Nadine Adler was next to them, though not sitting down. After last week when her growing belly kept her from getting up from her seated position on the floor, she'd gotten permission from Winston to stand, even though he was generally opposed to underlings standing in his presence. She shifted her weight from one leg to the other, clearly uncomfortable in whatever position she was in. The dark circles under her eyes were a testament to last night's lack of sleep as she tried to comfort Holly.

Kris Jingle was already dressed in Santa garb, for the first time in years actually looking happy to be there. Rumor was that Kris had a new girlfriend, and the other employees attributed that to his uncharacteristically jolly mood. The fact that his brother, Nicholas, was still sitting in jail for stealing Ralph's special Christmas piece last year and framing Kris for the theft certainly didn't seem to be dampening his spirits any.

As Winston approached the group, the mall employees murmured softly about the scowl on his face and the obvious irritation communicated by his stride. Whatever was upsetting him would certainly be taken out on the collective group.

"Good morning, troops!" Winston bellowed as he climbed the few stairs up to Santa's Workshop. "I hope you have your stations ready for the crowds that will descend upon us shortly. I know in these final days before Christmas, there is the tendency to slack off. It's completely normal to want a slower pace as we walk around with our favorite Christmas memories plaguing our minds. I want to remind you that this cannot be the case. We can't slow down, we must continue to advance even though the finish line is in sight. We must be at the ready to provide whatever our customers want. Is that understood?"

The employees nodded silently, each trying not to roll their eyes.

"I said, 'Is that understood?'" Winston barked at the unsatisfactory response.

"Yes, sir," they mumbled. It was a long-running joke that since Winston had received a medical discharge from the army while he was still in processing, he came back to Saddle Hill and treated his employees as though he was their commanding officer. Behind his back, they all called him "The General."

Seeming to accept their lackluster reply, he moved on to head count, which annoyed the business owners to their cores. Why did they have to be at these meetings, they'd often wondered, when they were paying Winston to rent space in his mall? Not to mention that they each paid their own employees from the profits their businesses made. All Winston did was own a building and rent the spaces out. He wasn't their boss, he depended on them to keep his job.

Mumbling each name under his breath, Winston went down the line. He seemed satisfied that everyone had reported for duty this morning.

As he began to descend the steps from Santa's Workshop, his head snapped up. His mouth was twisted into a grimace as he said in a low voice, "Where is Marian?" His eyes scanned the crowd again. His voice rose. "She isn't here. Where is she? She knows better than to leave Santa hanging in these final days before Christmas." His eyes shot toward Kris Jingle. "Do you know anything about this?"

Kris shook his head, and with furrowed brows scanned the small group of employees. "I haven't seen her since yesterday afternoon before the Christmas caroling," he offered. "Wait a minute. Holly isn't here either."

Winston's face flushed a deep shade of crimson. "Well,

where are they?" He shifted his eyes toward Ralph. "Where's Holly? Did you give her a day off?"

Ralph frowned. "No, and she didn't mention that she'd be late today, either."

Nadine raised her hand and said softly, "I spent the night with Holly last night. She barely slept a wink and isn't feeling like herself this morning. I'm not certain that she'll be in today at all," she looked toward Ralph, "but we all know she'll call you if she can't make it in."

Ralph nodded in understanding, but Winston seemed to blow a gasket. "You're telling me Holly is skipping out on work because she's tired from a slumber party? I understand she's still a young lady, but it's time she learned some responsibility and grew up a little."

Ralph cleared his throat. "Holly is my employee, not yours, and she has been a conscientious member of my staff for over a year. If she's not here, I know she has a good reason. Now, if you'll excuse me, I'm going to check on her." Ralph hoisted himself off the floor and strode quickly toward his store. On his way past Nadine, she grabbed his arm.

"Ralph, the reason Holly isn't here today is that she's worried sick about Marian," Nadine whispered.

"Marian? What happened to Marian? Is she okay?" Ralph asked, concern etched deep in his face.

"That's just it. We don't know where she is. She told Holly she had to run a quick errand after Christmas caroling, but she never made it home. Eli found her car abandoned near Henry Feinstein's house, but there was no sight of her. Apparently the driver's side door was standing open and the keys were still in the ignition. Eli and Joe have been out looking for her for hours but haven't found any sign of her."

Ralph's face went pale, and he covered his mouth with his hand. "What could have happened to her?"

Nadine chewed her thumbnail. "I wish I knew."

All Ralph and Nadine knew was that Marian Bright, the Christmas spirit of Saddle Hill, was missing.

CHAPTER ELEVEN

MARIAN SHIVERED UNDER a threadbare blanket in what appeared to be an old barn. Rusty milk cans were tossed haphazardly in the corner, old hoes, shovels, and rakes hung from hooks on the walls, and an ancient tiller half-covered by a grimy tarp occupied the middle of the room.

Squinting out the frost-covered window into the rising sun, Marian could see an old farmhouse in the distance, surrounded by a plank fence. Had this been a horse farm at one time? Marian wondered. From the peeling white paint on the house and the condition of the barn, it had obviously been neglected for many years. She didn't recognize the house, and guessed it was probably on the outskirts of town. There were so many little roads at the edge of town it was impossible to know where they all led and what was down each one.

Marian sighed. What was she doing here, trapped in an old barn with drafty windows and no insulation, when she should be winding down the season as Santa's helper?

Winter air poured through the cracks in the boards, which did little more than block the sharp gusts of wind. Curled into a tight ball on a pile of musty-smelling hay, Marian fought the urge to cry. Three days before Christmas, and here she was in a stinky, dilapidated barn instead of spreading holiday cheer.

What kind of cruel joke was this?

Marian closed her eyes, trying to remember what happened the night before. She'd been having a wonderful time caroling, then they were practically thrown off Henry Feinstein's property. She'd tried to talk to him, but he'd just become angrier.

Had he threatened her? Her brain was foggy about that.

Instead of going home to the party, she drove back to Henry's house to check on him. Everybody knew things had been tough for him since his wife died, and Roger's death was probably a blow to him as well. Roger had been the only friend who stuck by him through the drinking. No wonder he was angry. He probably feels like everyone he cared about left him.

I remember parking my car near his house, Marian thought, but what happened after that? The next thing I remember was waking up in this barn.

She pulled a hand out from under the blanket and rubbed it over her head, searching for any bumps or abrasions.

Nothing.

That's odd, Marian thought, furrowing her brows. I don't remember how I got here or seeing anyone when I got out of the car.

Was I drugged?

The thought made her shudder.

As she willed her mind to unlock the memory, the barn door creaked open, letting in a gust of frigid air.

"I brought some tea," a gruff voice said.

Marian opened her eyes and observed the man approaching her. He had broad shoulders and powerful arms that she had no doubt could hurt her if he tried. The thick beard added to the overall intimidating demeanor, but there was a softness in his eyes that communicated to Marian that he meant her no harm.

"Thank you," she said, successful in keeping her voice from shaking. She accepted the steaming mug of tea. Though relishing the warmth it provided, she coughed and sputtered as the bitter liquid went down her throat.

The man chuckled. "If you think that's bad, wait till you eat my cooking."

Marian scowled. "You know, it takes a special talent to mess up a cup of tea. All you have to do is dunk a tea bag in hot water for Pete's sake," she muttered as an idea sparked in her mind. Seizing the opportunity, she added, "My friends say I'm a good cook, and my Roger always raved about the big breakfasts I used to make for him—God rest his soul. And, not to brag, but I make the best hot chocolate in the world. Maybe you should let me do the cooking."

The man's eyes took on a wary look and he shook his head slightly. "I don't know if I'd be allowed to let you in the house. I can't make the boss mad. I'm on thin ice as it is."

Marian swallowed over the sudden constriction in her throat. *Boss?*

She took another sip of the tea and coughed. "Well, if your cooking is as bad as your tea, you might be in more danger of food poisoning than whatever your boss would do to you."

The bearded man laughed softly. "You might be right." He paused in thought. "I'll tell ya what. I'll think about letting you come inside, but you'd have to promise not to make trouble."

Hope soaring, Marian thanked the man.

"I said I'd think about it. That doesn't mean 'yes.'"

"Of course," she replied, trying to keep the excitement out of her voice.

The man nodded slightly toward Marian then walked toward the door he'd come through just minutes ago. "I'll be out with breakfast in an hour," he said as he pulled the door closed behind him.

As she listened to the lock engage, a wave of desperation washed over Marian. Someone had ordered her kidnapping, and this guy was just doing that person's bidding.

But who would want to have her kidnapped? And why?

CHAPTER TWELVE

VITO FRANKS PUTTERED around the kitchen of the old farmhouse he'd be calling home for the near future. He wasn't exactly used to the finer things in life, but this place was the pits. The cracked linoleum floors creaked under his feet, the countertops were peeling, and an odor hung in the air that told him that at some point, a creature had died in here.

And that was just the kitchen. The rest of the house was just as bad. The bathroom had rust stains in the sink, toilet, and on the bottom of the shower. All the furniture was lumpy and smelled of dust and mildew.

It's a real shame, too, he thought as he scrambled a few eggs and buttered a piece of burnt toast. This place could be beautiful if it were just given a little time and care.

The carpenter in him itched to restore the place to its former charm. Unfortunately, that wasn't the job he'd been hired to do. Desperate times called for desperate actions, so when he was approached about kidnapping this old lady, he'd agreed, thinking only of the financial windfall coming his way.

Drugging her seemed the best way to keep her from

struggling. While chloroform was a cliché when it came to rendering a victim unconscious, it seemed like the safest and best option. That was the only option his boss had given him, other than wrestling the woman into his truck. The roads and sidewalks had been slick last night, and he just didn't have it in him to risk injuring himself or her. Judging by what he saw of her just a little while ago, he realized chloroform was a good call. She was a spunky little thing and could very well have caused them both to get hurt on the ice.

He settled at the wobbly kitchen table with the breakfast he'd just prepared and took a bite of the toast. It crunched against his teeth. The charred flavor reminded him of the smell of smoke that billowed out of his childhood home when he'd been playing with matches.

That house had burned to the ground.

Dropping his toast on the plate, he scooped up a forkful of scrambled eggs. They were cold and gelatinous in his mouth. He spit them back onto his plate and thought longingly about the breakfasts his mom used to cook on Saturday mornings, complete with fried potatoes, scrambled eggs, sausage, cheese grits, and blueberry muffins. Then for dinner they'd either have beef stew and biscuits or fried pork chops, mashed potatoes, and green beans cooked in bacon grease.

No wonder both my parents died early of heart attacks, he mused, then clicked on the old TV that sat on a stool in the corner of the room. Turning it to the news, he listened as the mayor urgently communicated that tonight would be the coldest night in a decade, with the windchill falling below negative-ten. "Bring your pets inside," she said, "and make sure any farm animals are protected from the wind. Leaving them outside on a night like this will be a death sentence."

A death sentence.

Vito's eyes swept in the direction of the barn. His gut clenched. He couldn't leave that woman out there. She'd freeze to death. He might have recently become a kidnapper-for-hire, but he certainly couldn't let her die. Chewing on his bottom lip, he wondered if he should even bother to mention to the boss that he was going to bring the lady inside.

His father's voice echoed in his head. *Better to ask for forgiveness than permission.* That was a motto his dad had lived and died by and it had gotten him into more trouble than he ever admitted. From the stories he'd heard from his grandmother, living that way had even landed Vito senior in jail a time or two.

Like father, like son…

If he ever got caught.

The thought of a decent home-cooked meal made his mouth water. Nervous fingers drummed the table. No matter what, he couldn't let anything happen to the woman. He was many things that he wasn't proud of, but a killer wasn't one of them.

Mind made up, he stood, the legs of the chair scraping the warped floor as he did. He'd do his best to make sure nothing happened to her, and if he just happened to get some good food out of the deal—well, that would make saving her life even better.

CHAPTER THIRTEEN

A GRIM GROUP of Saddle Hill Mall employees gathered around a corner table at the Rose Petal Café. Looking gloomier than anyone had ever seen him, James Jingle stared into his cup of coffee muttering, "How could something happen to a person like Marian? She's such a role model to us all…"

Holly Berry sniffed quietly and dabbed at her eyes with a tissue. Gulping loudly, she lamented, "How could I have not noticed sooner that Marian wasn't there last night? She was gone two hours before I even said anything. If something happened to her, I'll never be able to forgive myself." A sob broke free from her throat.

Nadine, who'd been approaching the table with a tray of muffins, set it down and put a comforting arm around Holly. "None of this is your fault, Holly. Nobody noticed Marian wasn't at the party. We were all too wrapped up in our own business to pay much attention. The only reason we found out she was missing was because of you. You're the one that told Eli she wasn't there, and it was because of you that they went looking for her," she said tenderly. She squeezed Holly into a tight hug, then released her.

The group nodded and murmured its agreement, but Holly only sniffed more.

"Well, I for one won't rest until we find her," Ralph Stockton announced. "Marian is one of our own, and we can't give up on her."

Ralph Stockton, now financially secure—and much to Winston's dismay—had closed his store for the day. Always good friends with Marian, and especially fond of her after she helped identify the thief that nearly ruined his business last Christmas, he couldn't stand idly by while the sheriff and his deputy searched.

Sylvia Bell, looking chic even in her flannel shirt and ponytail, nodded in agreement. "I know I haven't known her as long as you all have, but in this last year she has become very dear to me. I want to help however I can, too."

Wearing his familiar scowl, Sheriff Joe Adler trudged into the Rose Petal Café, Deputy Eli Nolan following behind.

Nadine distanced herself from the group and met him before he reached them. "Anything?" she asked in a hushed tone.

Joe's mouth tightened. He shook his head.

"Where could she be?" Nadine whispered.

"I don't know. We're searching the best we can, but there are so many out-of-the-way places around Saddle Hill that it's going to take a lot of time with just me and Eli."

Holly stood, stepping into Eli's arms. As she rested her head on his shoulder, the small crowd heard her muffled words. "Where could she be? There's no way Marian would wander off on her own. Especially at Christmas."

Eli smoothed Holly's long red hair, looked down into her tear-filled eyes, and said, "We'll find her. I promise."

Silence settled over the group as they tried to process what Christmas in Saddle Hill would be like without their resident elf there to share it with them.

As they were each occupied by their own thoughts, a woman with waist-length, raven-colored hair, accompanied by a man with a camera, walked into the café.

Joe raised an eyebrow. "I wonder what they want," he whispered to Nadine.

Following Joe's gaze, Nadine said, "I don't know, but it looks like Marian's disappearance is about to hit the news."

CHAPTER FOURTEEN

CAROL LING WALKED with her back straight into the Rose Petal Café. Followed by Hank, her cameraman, she had every intention of getting the reaction of the townspeople as footage for the six o'clock news.

Working for a station like WGNN—*We're the Good News Network*—meant that she covered plenty of heartwarming stories that were aimed at giving the public something other than war, famine, and disease to focus on. The mission of the network was to give viewers a much-needed break from the harsh realities of global heartache. While she didn't have a chance to cover the hard-hitting news stories that some of her friends from college did, she'd spent her career as a journalist curling up in bed every night feeling good about humanity. Even so, it was sometimes hard to be the butt of the joke around other reporters.

Add her name to the mix, and she'd become used to being made fun of.

Throughout her growing-up years, her classmates would start singing Christmas carols anytime she entered the room or got out of her seat to throw away a piece of trash. For years, she'd struggled with resenting her parents for sticking her with a name like "Carol Ling." Fortunately for her, that very name made a great byline for a company like WGNN.

It had been a stroke of luck to stumble across an online chat room dedicated to people with Christmas names. It was there that she'd seen posts from Marian Bright and Holly Berry about the first-annual winter solstice caroling event. It became clear that Marian had a Christmas spirit like few others, and when Carol pitched the idea of doing a feature story on Saddle Hill, her boss had been delighted that one town could be the home of so much good news.

It had also been a stroke of luck that one of Saddle Hill's most beloved citizens had gone missing. Not that she wanted harm to come to anyone. Quite the contrary. There was a reason she, for the most part, genuinely enjoyed her job at WGNN. But Marian's disappearance could be the break she was looking for. Maybe now other journalists would start taking her seriously.

First, though, she'd have to nail these interviews with the townspeople who were gathered around the table.

Pushing her shoulders back, she strode toward the small group, intent on doing the best piece of reporting she'd ever done.

❧

"Hi. I'm not sure if you remember me. My name is Carol Ling with WGNN. I was out caroling with you all last night," she said once she'd reached the group. "I'm covering the disappearance of Marian Bright, and I wonder if each of you might consent to an interview."

She watched as Marian's friends shared puzzled looks with one another.

"My goal is to reach as many people as I can in hopes that somebody, somewhere has information about her whereabouts." Carol paused and held her breath. As much as she wanted the credit for covering Marian's safe return, she was completely dependent on the locals for help.

After exchanging wary glances with one another, a pretty woman in her early forties said, "Of course. We'll do anything we can to help bring Marian home. She's like family to us… to all of us."

Carol fought the urge to express her glee, and instead said, "Great. Can I ask your name?"

The woman nodded a head covered in wavy brown locks, pulled into a ponytail. "Sylvia Bell. I'm a part-time resident of Saddle Hill."

Despite the hairdo and the flannel shirt she wore, there was something undeniably classy about the woman. She'll look great on camera, Carol thought. "Wonderful," she said. "Would you all mind if I had Hank, my cameraman, film you while you talk about Marian and what she means to this community?"

Several folks murmured, "Of course." Carol had a hunch that the people in this group were the ones closest to Marian.

"Since you agreed first," Carol said, looking toward Sylvia, "would you be willing to tell us more about what Marian means to you, personally?"

Nodding toward Hank, she was rewarded by the flashing red light that indicated the camera was now recording. Speaking directly at the camera, she said, "I'm here with Sylvia Bell, a resident of Saddle Hill where the local spirit of Christmas,

Marian Bright, has gone missing." Carol turned toward Sylvia and said, "Ms. Bell, can you please share with us how the disappearance of Marian Bright has affected you personally?"

Sylvia looked at the camera, her face solemn. "I think I can speak for the entire town when I say we are all incredibly worried about Marian and are absolutely certain she would never simply take off without saying a word to anyone."

Carol spoke clearly, projecting her voice toward the microphone attached to the camera. "You have mentioned to me that you're only a part-time resident of Saddle Hill. How long have you known Ms. Bright?"

"I only met Marian last Christmas, but she quickly became like family to me." Sylvia motioned toward the rest of the group. "She's like family to all of us."

"Thank you, Ms. Bell." She waved a hand toward the others gathered at the table. "Would any of you like to say something to Marian, if she's watching, or to the person who might be responsible for helping her disappear?"

Ralph Stockton rose to his feet. "Who *helped* her disappear?" he said angrily. "I'll tell you this right now, Marian didn't want to disappear. If someone is involved in *making* her disappear, she went with them involuntarily. That's something we're all sure of." Without another word, Ralph strode out of the café and walked toward his store. Though it was closed for business the rest of the day, it would provide a quiet place for him to think—and worry.

From behind the camera, Hank shot Carol a questioning look and mouthed, "What now?"

Before Carol had a chance to respond, a young woman with shimmering red hair cleared her throat. She clenched a wadded tissue in one hand and brushed the hair out of her face with the other. "Marian has been like a grandmother to me. She gave me a new start when my life was in the dumps. Without any other family I could count on, Marian took me under her wing and welcomed me into her life and her home. The only thing we know is that this year, Christmas won't be the same if Marian isn't home." Tears filled Holly's eyes again, and she looked back at the camera. "Please, to everyone watching, help us get Marian home in time for Christmas."

CHAPTER FIFTEEN

MARIAN SCRUBBED THE cracked Formica countertop with a scouring pad and sighed. This place was a mess. While she was glad to not be stuck in the drafty old barn anymore, she knew she couldn't stay in this house in its current shape. Since it was obvious she wouldn't be getting away from here whenever she wanted, it needed to feel like a temporary home away from home.

After trying the locks to see if there was a way to escape, she found that she was locked in from the outside and could only get out if she had the key. The windows wouldn't budge either, so for the time being, she was stuck.

Might as well make the best of it, she'd told herself, and got to work tidying up. The kitchen was almost finished, the warped linoleum floors now shone brightly and smelled of pine. The counter and sink, scoured with an industrial-strength chemical, now had only faint traces of the dark stains that had marred them earlier.

Her kidnapper sat back and watched, his eyes shining with amusement. "What's the point in cleaning up this old house?"

he'd asked her more than once. After pointing out to her that it wasn't her responsibility—his either, for that matter—he'd suggested that she just let it go. The homeowner didn't care, so why should she?

Marian had explained to him that the kitchen was the heart of the home, and since she'd be spending most of her time in there, she wanted it to be clean. After all, she had big plans for cooking and baking while she was here. It was still the Christmas season, and even though she couldn't be home, she intended to celebrate anyway.

After rinsing the scouring pad and placing it next to the sink to dry, she grabbed a pad of paper and pen that had been sitting on a nearby table and began scratching out a detailed store list. She might not be able to go herself, but her kidnapper could. She could tell that he wanted a decent, home-cooked meal. By letting her out of the barn and into the house without permission, he'd already shown he'd go against the "boss" to make sure he got it.

Humming Christmas carols as she wrote, she suddenly felt the weight of eyes staring at her. When she raised her head to meet those of her captor, she smiled faintly, then continued humming.

"You really love Christmas, don't you?" he asked.

"Of course. Don't you?"

He shrugged. "I used to. When I was a kid. Once my mom and dad died, the holidays became less special."

Marian placed the pen on the notepad and turned in her chair to face the man. "Have you been alone all this time?"

Shaking his head, the man dropped his eyes to his hands. "I had a wife once, and kids. She took up with some big-city lawyer a few years ago and I haven't seen her or my kids since."

Marian reached toward him and clasped his hand in hers. It was a rough, calloused hand that suggested a life of hard labor. "I'm so sorry," she said. "I lost my Roger eighteen months ago. This is my second Christmas without him. Fortunately, I've got some great friends who have welcomed me into their lives. It has helped ease the pain of losing him."

The man snorted and rubbed his beard. "Lucky you. Unfortunately, I found out what kind of friends I really had when they all stopped coming around. Then it got hard to find work, and here we are. You can guess the rest."

Marian pinched her lips together and nodded. So this guy really is just the hired gun, she thought. He never meant me any harm, he just needed a paycheck.

Feeling a stab of pity for the man, she said, "You know what? I'm going to make you the best dinner you ever had tonight. But you'll need to go to the store… unless you want me to do it."

A smile parted the man's lips. "Nice try. I'd be a goner if I let you out of here."

Marian shrugged. "It was worth a try." She picked up the pen and kept making her list. She'd make her well-loved potpie, spiced cider, and bourbon bread pudding for dessert. She tapped her chin with the pen and smiled. Maybe some hot buttered rum, too.

Hopeful that her secret ingredients would tip off the grocer, she dispatched her kidnapper with the list.

"Don't try anything," he gently warned as he walked out the front door.

As the door clicked shut, Marian chewed on her lip. Even if the grocer didn't notice her secret ingredients, maybe she'd be able to get her kidnapper to drink enough rum that it would be easy to persuade him to let her go. If not, she could at least get him talking enough to find out why she was here.

Her gut told her this guy wasn't bad but had just fallen on hard times. If she could get him to open up to her, she might have hope of finding out who was behind this kidnapping and figure out a way to signal for help.

CHAPTER SIXTEEN

"SO, WHAT DID you think of that reporter?" Eli asked Joe once they were back at the station.

Joe shrugged. "She seemed like most reporters, like she cared more about getting the story than about truly helping us find Marian."

"You could have said something to her," Eli suggested.

Huffing his displeasure, Joe said, "The last thing this town needs is law enforcement getting on camera when we have absolutely no leads on what happened to Marian. Small-town cops already have a reputation as being Barney Fife replicas. We don't need to help reinforce that stereotype."

Joe studied Eli. To Joe, he almost looked like a kid playing dress-up in his dad's uniform. In the sheriff station, complete with wood paneling and deer heads mounted on the wall, Eli looked out of place. He was a good guy, but young. At twenty-four years old, he still had a lot to learn about reading people. Even with a job in law enforcement, he remained unjaded when it came to his view of humanity.

Maybe he should have worked security at the mall, Joe

mused. Having a boss like Winston Marshall was enough to change his view of people. Not to mention working with the public every day. Most of the time they were okay, but once the Christmas season rolled around, it seemed as though everyone turned into materialistic grumps. More than once he'd had to break up fights when there was only one of something left. Even though no one had paid for it and it still belonged to the store, these people would stake claim to it as if it was their own personal possession.

He shook his head, reliving the days he felt more like a bouncer at a bar than mall security. This job was much better. The hours were less stable and the crimes more serious than somebody getting smacked with an oversized handbag in a scuffle for the last stuffed animal for a grandkid, but at least he felt like he was making a difference. Now he was only called to help when people were past the point of helping themselves.

"Whatcha thinking of over there?" Eli asked as he polished his firearm.

Joe watched Eli for a few minutes before answering. It seemed like Eli was always cleaning his firearm. He said it helped him think.

"I was just thinking about when I worked security at the mall, and the way people acted around the holidays," Joe finally answered.

Laying the pistol on his desk, Eli studied Joe with intense brown eyes, then said, "Do you think that difference in attitude during the holidays has something to do with Marian's disappearance?"

Scratching his chin, Joe admitted he hadn't considered it. If his job in security at the mall taught him anything, it was that people were capable of acting out of character if it meant getting something they wanted. "If so, that would definitely suggest that someone is behind Marian's disappearance and she didn't leave on her own accord. I guess it's always a possibility." He raked his fingers through his hair. "But Marian is a retired schoolteacher who now works as a mall elf. The only thing she's ever done is teach kids or make them smile at Christmastime. Certainly no one would have hurt her, right?" he thought aloud.

"That's what we need to find out."

"You're right." Joe stood and stuffed his arms into his winter jacket. "What are we doing sitting around here? Let's get out there and chase down some leads."

As the two men walked out into the snow to Joe's cruiser, Joe racked his brain about who could be responsible for taking Marian, if that was actually what had happened. As they slipped into the car, Joe played the events of the last two days in his mind, remembering an altercation from the night before.

"Eli, I think we need to pay Henry Feinstein a visit," Joe said grimly.

Henry Feinstein had been openly hostile toward Marian when they were Christmas caroling, and it was no secret that he had a volatile temper. His stint in jail for assault proved that. If Marian had gone back to his house in an effort to talk to him, as the location of her abandoned car suggested, could Henry have lost his temper and lashed out at her?

A sinking feeling settled in Joe's stomach. With a predisposition toward violence, if Henry had been drinking heavily before Marian went to see him, who knows what he could have done to her.

<h1 style="text-align:center">CHAPTER SEVENTEEN</h1>

NADINE SLID A cup of chamomile tea in front of Holly and settled into the chair next to her, then reached over to give Holly's hand a squeeze. "We'll find her," Nadine said, hoping her words were true. "Joe and Eli won't rest until they have her back home, safe and sound."

Fresh tears sprang to Holly's eyes and she quickly blinked them away. "You know, before I met Marian, I felt completely alone. I didn't belong anywhere or with anybody. When my parents split, they couldn't even be civil with each other. It got to the point where the only time they'd speak to me was to complain about the other one. As soon as I was old enough, I left home and never looked back. Marian became the only family I had. She never judged me for my past or expected me to be anything different than what I was. All I ever got from her was love. Now she's gone." A sob escaped Holly's throat as a few fat tears plopped onto her jeans, leaving dark spots where they landed.

Placing a comforting arm around Holly's shoulder, Nadine pulled her close. "I know," she soothed. "We have no evidence that anything bad has happened to Marian. If her car slid off the road, she could have bumped her head and gotten confused, then started wandering around. Joe told me they had her car towed to the station, and they didn't find any trace of blood."

Holly shuddered, then sniffed. "I guess that's a good thing."

Nadine nodded in agreement. "It's a very good thing." She paused and added, "Marian isn't your only family anymore. You've got a whole lot of us that think of you as family. You're the little sister I never had, and Joe is like your ornery brother-in-law. I know Ralph and Carla care about you like parents would. Please stop telling yourself you're alone in this world."

"Thank you for reminding me and thank you for leaving the café to be with me," Holly said, wiping her eyes with the tissue she kept in the pocket of her jeans.

"No problem. This little guy keeps me pretty worn out, so I could use the day off," Nadine replied, rubbing her hand in a circle on her basketball-shaped belly. "I'm sure Winston will be furious and never let me hear the end of it, though."

Holly raised the mug to take a sip of tea, but her hand stopped midair when the doorbell rang.

"I wonder who that could be," Nadine murmured, then placed her own mug back on the table. She walked to the front door to answer it and came back to the kitchen with Sylvia Bell at her side.

"I just wanted to stop by and check on you," Sylvia said, the dark circles under her eyes a stark contrast to her otherwise flawless complexion.

"Thank you. I'm doing okay, considering. It would be much worse if I didn't have the two of you to remind me I'm not alone," Holly said, giving Sylvia a watery smile.

As Sylvia looked around at the festively decorated house,

Nadine could tell what she was thinking. She'd had the same thought she could now see on Sylvia's face. No matter how much the house was decorated for Christmas, Marian's absence was felt, and the festive decor fell flat. It was almost as though Marian took the spirit of Christmas with her when she disappeared.

"Well, I for one don't plan to sit around here and wait for Joe and Eli to find her," Sylvia announced. "They're not the only ones that can get things done around here."

Holly's head snapped up from staring into her tea. Nadine arched an eyebrow at her.

"What did you have in mind?" Nadine asked.

"We were all with Marian last night before she disappeared. And Holly, you know Marian better than anybody. If we work together, I'm sure we can find out what happened to her," Sylvia urged.

The confidence in her voice bolstered Nadine's. "You're right. Holly, you know Marian's routine. You'll have information nobody else does. Get your boots and coat, we're heading out."

"But won't Joe and Eli be mad?" Holly fretted.

Nadine shrugged. "If they are, they are. We'll deal with that when we have to. Right now, finding Marian is priority one."

Sylvia laughed. "Nadine, you're starting to sound like Joe."

Covering her mouth with one hand, Nadine blushed. "I am, aren't I?" she said, then straightened her back. "Well, in the spirit of my husband, let's go find Marian."

As their boots crunched on the snow blanketing the driveway, Nadine couldn't help but wonder if this was a good idea. If Marian didn't just wander off, if she were *taken*, what would happen to the three of them if they did find the person responsible?

CHAPTER EIGHTEEN

JOE BANGED HIS fist against the front door of Henry Feinstein's house. "Open up, Feinstein! Sheriff Adler and Deputy Nolan here to talk to you."

"Think he'll answer the door?" Eli asked.

"He'd better."

A crash came from inside the house, followed by several others. "What in the world?" Joe muttered.

A minute later, a bleary-eyed Henry Feinstein opened the door, looking—and smelling—as though he hadn't showered in a week. "Whaddya want?" he slurred.

"You doing okay today, Henry?" Eli asked, amused. The only times he'd ever met Henry Feinstein—other than Christmas caroling last night—was responding to calls about drunken disorderlies.

"Just fine," Henry growled. "What are you doing on my property?"

Eli, whose approach was a bit softer than Joe's, began to speak, but was immediately cut off.

"Did you see Marian Bright last night?" Joe asked, a sharp edge in his voice.

Henry Feinstein wobbled and grasped the doorframe. "Yeah, I saw her. She was singing out here with a bunch of other trespassers."

"After that. Did you see her again later after everybody else was gone?" Eli pressed, taking his cue from Joe.

Henry turned his attention to Eli and tilted his head. "Aren't you a little young for this job?"

Eli stiffened. "I'm plenty old enough for this job. Now answer the question."

A sideways glance at Joe revealed that he was trying not to smile. Eli knew why. Ever since Joe was elected sheriff, he'd been telling Eli that he was too soft, that he needed to be a little tougher with people. Joe's hidden smile was his way of approving of the way Eli was handling the situation.

"Nah. I never saw her again after that," Henry finally said. "What's it matter, anyway?"

Eli took a step closer. "Why don't you take a shower and put on something decent. You smell like you spent the night inside a whiskey bottle."

"You can't tell me what to do, boy," Henry growled, taking a shaky step forward.

Joe placed a restraining hand on Henry's chest before he was able to close the distance between them any more. "Do as Deputy Nolan said. We've got some questions for you, and you stink too bad to talk to. Maybe run a toothbrush over those grimy teeth while you're at it."

Snorting his disapproval, Henry Feinstein turned and stumbled toward the stairs to the right of the front door.

"That guy's gonna break his neck on those steps," Eli muttered.

Joe shrugged. "The world's lost better people, that's for sure." Stepping over the threshold, he motioned for Eli to follow him. "We'll wait inside. There's no reason for us to get frostbite out here while he takes his sweet time making himself presentable. Though that might take a miracle," Joe added.

As they entered the cluttered house, Eli took note that there were almost no personal touches to the place. There wasn't a single Christmas decoration to be seen, and the floor was littered with empty liquor bottles. He kicked one out of his way as he walked to a small table under the window that held a single framed picture. Though the room was dimly lit, he could see that it was a photo of two people on their wedding day. The woman smiled radiantly as she looked at her groom. The man's arm circled her waist, pulling her close as he nuzzled his face into her hair. In the picture, it looked as though the two were very much in love. Eli took a step toward the table and bent lower to get a closer look. If he didn't know any better, he'd swear the man was Henry Feinstein.

"Take a look at this," Joe said, pulling Eli from his thoughts.

Eli turned to see Joe stooped over a drawer, rifling through some papers. "Do you think you ought to be doing that? We don't have a warrant," Eli warned.

Joe stood, his hand clutching several papers. "Do you really think Feinstein will notice? The man doesn't stay sober long enough to know what's here and what's not."

Intrigued, Eli closed the gap between him and Joe. "What did you find?"

"I can't be sure, exactly, but it looks like a property map."

"So?"

"So, if he did something to Marian, we might find her there," Joe suggested.

The sound of someone coming down the stairs behind them made both men turn around to face a showered and shaved Henry Feinstein. With clearer speech, Henry said, "What were you guys asking me?"

Joe held up the papers he was holding. "I think we should talk at the station."

Despite his protests, Henry followed them to the vehicle and climbed in the back.

Henry might have the information they need to find Marian, Eli thought. If so, he'd make Holly the happiest girl in the world by returning Marian home by sundown.

CHAPTER NINETEEN

VITO FRANKS PUSHED the shopping cart around the small grocery store as he searched for the items on Marian's list. He kept his hat pulled low on his forehead and his head slightly ducked in hopes that nobody would notice him.

To Vito's surprise, everyone that did manage to make eye contact greeted him with a warm smile and wished him a Merry Christmas.

If they only knew the secret I'm carrying, he thought, guilt threatening to overtake him.

There was no doubt word had spread around town about Marian Bright's disappearance, and everyone was probably worried sick about her. They wouldn't be nearly so friendly if they knew he was the reason she was missing.

Squelching the urge to drive back to the farmhouse and let Marian go, he reminded himself that if the boss wanted Marian to be kidnapped, there were a lot worse people out there that would have been more than willing to take care of it. Unfortunately, most of those people would have also been more than willing to do whatever it took to keep her quiet… and to avoid getting caught.

Yep. There was no doubt about it: Marian was safer with him.

Once he'd gotten everything he needed for the potpie, cider, and hot buttered rum, among other things, Vito made his way to the checkout.

A friendly man wearing a name tag that said "Fred" greeted him and began scanning the groceries. After the obligatory greetings, Vito tried to discourage any further conversation.

No luck.

"It looks like you've got the makings of a fine dinner," Fred observed and continued scanning. "Hmmm. On a night as cold as tonight is supposed to be, you'll be glad about the cider. Oh, and I see you've got plans for hot buttered rum."

Vito fought the urge to yell at the man to shut up, and instead dug several twenty-dollar bills out of his wallet. The last thing he needed was to get everyone's attention… especially for an angry outburst.

Fred pressed a few buttons on the cash register and pulled out the receipt. He handed it to Vito and said, "Merry Christmas. Enjoy your dinner." Then, with a furrowed brow, he added, "You know, there's only one other person I know that uses dried cranberries and cinnamon sticks in her hot buttered rum. I thought her recipe was a secret, one-of-a-kind, but I guess not. Looks like she might be onto something, though."

With a tight smile, Vito thanked Fred and walked out into the cold. Now he could only hope that his new buddy Fred didn't put two and two together and go running his mouth to the sheriff about a stranger that came into the store, buying the same ingredients that Marian Bright used in her top-secret, one-of-a-kind, hot buttered rum.

CHAPTER TWENTY

THE BACK END of the car fishtailed on the snowy road as Sylvia, Nadine, and Holly drove down a picturesque country lane in search of Marian. Joe had told Nadine last night that Marian's car had been abandoned outside Henry Feinstein's house, but she could be anywhere by now.

Holly's phone pinged, indicating she'd just gotten a text message.

"Listen!" Holly shouted from the backseat.

The car swerved and Sylvia threw her arm across the passenger seat where Nadine was sitting. "Hold on ladies," Sylvia said. "These roads are terrible. I don't think the plows come out this far."

"Sorry for startling you," Holly apologized, her stomach up near her throat after what felt like two close calls in a row. "I just got a text from Eli. He said he and Joe took Henry Feinstein into the station for questioning. They suspect he might have taken Marian."

Nadine's head whipped around. "I don't know that Eli

should have told you that. Joe always says they can't talk about ongoing investigations."

Holly shrugged. "He knows how worried I am about Marian. I think he's just trying to keep me informed so I know they're working on it."

"We're all worried about Marian," Sylvia interjected, keeping her eyes firmly focused on the road ahead. "Don't let Eli do anything to jeopardize the investigation just so you can feel like you know what's going on. The most important thing is for us to get her back."

Holly slunk back in the seat and crossed her arms like a child who'd just been scolded. "He was just trying to make me feel better," she muttered in a tone that communicated her annoyance with the two women in the front of the car.

"I don't know that getting information that Marian may have been kidnapped makes anyone feel better," Nadine said, her heart obviously heavy with worry about their missing friend.

"Well, we're not going to leave it all to Joe and Eli," Sylvia said and guided the car down a long, narrow driveway that led to a neglected old farmhouse.

"Here it goes," Sylvia breathed as she parked the car and unbuckled. Holly and Nadine did the same, and the three of them walked toward the porch together.

Holly, armed with a picture of Marian smiling for the camera dressed in her elf regalia, knocked on the door.

A minute later, the door was answered by a bearded man with a nose that was red from the cold. "Can I help you?" he asked in a gruff voice.

Thrusting the picture in front of the man's face, Holly asked, "Have you seen Marian?"

"I don't know anyone named Marian," he replied, then took a step back and narrowed his eyes. "You're missing an elf?"

"No," Holly said impatiently. "We're missing our friend, Marian. She works as an elf at the mall during the Christmas season. Have you seen her?"

"Afraid not. We don't get many visitors way out here."

Tears stung the backs of Holly's eyes. "I see. Well, if you do see her, will you make sure to call the sheriff? We miss her."

"Sure thing, ma'am," the man said.

Nadine and Sylvia murmured their thanks as the trio turned and trudged back toward the car.

"This woman that's missing," the man called from the porch. "Does she have any health problems that would put her in danger out there?"

Holly turned and shook her head. "She's healthier than all of us put together. She has more energy, too."

The man nodded in understanding then clicked the door shut, leaving the three women to wonder if there was any hope of finding Marian before the temperature dropped tonight.

CHAPTER TWENTY-ONE

VITO FRANKS WALKED into the kitchen where Marian was busily putting the finishing touches on the potpie before popping it into the oven.

"An elf?" he asked her, raising one eyebrow, his eyes shining with amusement.

"What?"

"You're an elf?"

A smile crinkled the skin around Marian's pale blue eyes. "For one month a year, I'm a mall elf, yes."

Stroking his beard, Vito studied her. "I could see that."

He was already growing to enjoy the company of his captive, but his increasing sense of remorse for taking her away from family and friends gnawed at him. "Some people were here looking for you."

Marian finished cutting an 'x' in the top crust of the potpie and whipped around to face him. "They were? Who?"

Vito shrugged. "Three ladies."

"What did they look like?" Marian urged.

"The one who did all the talking was a pretty little thing

with long red hair. Another one looked like she was pregnant, but I know you're not supposed to ask women those kinds of things. The other was a real beauty. Didn't look like she belonged here," he volunteered.

"Holly, Nadine, and Sylvia," Marian murmured. "Did they seem okay? What about the pregnant one? Did she seem to be in any pain or discomfort?"

Vito raised a shoulder and let it drop. "I guess she looked fine. I'd say somebody as far along as her must be uncomfortable all the time. That's how it was for my wife, anyway. She never let me hear the end of it." A shadow of pain flickered across Vito's face, then disappeared. "Looks like you have people that really care about you."

Marian smiled again. "I do. We all look out for each other."

Taking a small step toward Marian, Vito said, "I'm sorry Christmas is working out like this for you this year."

Nodding, Marian said, "My Roger always loved gardening. When he'd hear someone complaining about their life and wishing it was different, he'd always say to them, 'Grow where you're planted.' For right now, I'm planted here. I might as well make the best of it. Besides, the silver lining is that I get to keep you company and you don't have to spend Christmas alone."

Vito nodded and hung his head. "I'm sorry. Being with me at Christmas isn't much of a silver lining," he murmured, then left the room.

Walking to what he assumed used to be an office, he settled into a sagging and dusty upholstered chair. His head in his hands, he loathed the day he ever agreed to this plan. No amount of money was worth hurting this nice woman. People missed her, and she clearly missed them, even though she was trying to "grow where she was planted." That she would even consider it a positive thing that she got to keep him company this Christmas was a testament to a goodwill that he thought was long gone from the human race.

He had to make this right. But how could he free Marian without the boss finding out? Even though there hadn't been any direct threats of physical harm, he sensed that the person pulling the strings would stop at nothing to make sure the plan was fulfilled.

Gritting his teeth, Vito vowed to himself and to Marian that he'd do whatever was necessary to make sure Marian made it out of this dump and was home before Christmas.

But how?

CHAPTER TWENTY-TWO

HENRY FEINSTEIN SHIFTED uncomfortably in his chair in the interview room at the sheriff station. "Why'd ya have to bring me here?" he complained as he scratched his freshly shaved jaw.

"Because we need to talk to you about Marian Bright," Joe said.

"What about her?"

Joe leaned back in his chair and crossed his arms over his chest. "You tell me."

"Tell you what? There's nothing to tell," Henry countered.

"Let me refresh your memory," Joe said, leaning forward and placing his elbows on the table between him and his suspect. "Last night you had some pretty harsh words for Marian while she was Christmas caroling at your house. Some witnesses said they thought it sounded like a threat. This morning, she's missing, and her car was found on the street in front of your house. Sound familiar?"

A horrified expression filled Henry's eyes. "Marian is missing?"

A silent nod was Joe's only reaction.

"I was there," Eli interjected. "You told Marian she'd be sorry she bothered you. Sounds like a threat to me. What did you do to make her sorry?"

Henry shifted in his chair again. "Nothing!" he objected. "I swear to you I didn't do anything to Marian. Those were just words. Words don't mean nothing."

Joe nodded and slid a piece of paper across the table toward Henry. "Tell me about this."

"Where'd you get that?" Henry demanded, pointing to the property map that was now between the men.

"I did a little looking around when you were getting yourself cleaned up." He pointed to the paper. "Looks like you've got some property way out on the outskirts of town. Want to tell me about it?"

Red crept up Henry's neck and found his cheeks. "You got no right to be looking through my things without a warrant. That paper is none of your business."

Joe snorted. "If you don't have anything to hide, why don't you tell me about this property?"

Shaking his head fervently, Henry said, "No way. I want a lawyer. You're going to try to pin something on me. That's what always happens. You want information about that," he said, pointing to the property map, "you're going to have to go through a lawyer."

"Way to make yourself look more guilty, Feinstein," Joe snapped, then pushed back his chair from the table and strode out of the room.

Eli watched his partner's back as he retreated, then, his voice softer, said, "Look, Henry. I know you were drunk last night when you were making those threats, but it still looks bad. Real bad." He held up his hand and ticked off his points one by one. "You made threats against Marian, her car was found abandoned in front of your house, and now she's missing. Not to mention you have land right smack in the middle of nowhere where you could stash Marian—or her body. Help us out and tell us about this property."

Henry's mouth formed a hard, straight line. "If you want anything from me, you can talk to my lawyer." His fiery gaze communicated that playing good cop wouldn't get Eli anywhere with Henry Feinstein.

"Have it your way," Eli muttered, then stood and left the room.

Looks like Marian won't be home tonight, after all, he thought, wondering how he would be able to break the news to Holly and hoping the information he slipped to her about Henry Feinstein being a suspect in Marian's disappearance hadn't already compromised the investigation.

CHAPTER TWENTY-THREE

FRED ROONEY SIPPED his coffee in the employee break room at the Saddle Hill Market. Something was bugging him, but he couldn't quite put his finger on it. It had something to do with a customer he'd had earlier in the day, but with most of the town out picking up last-minute groceries for their Christmas feasts, the whole morning had passed in a blur.

He'd worked at the market for decades and knew everyone in town. Sometimes he talked to people too much and it made his lines go slower, but the customers didn't seem to mind. In fact, it was one of the things that made small-town life so special. With a slower pace, people had time to visit. Fred just couldn't understand how people in bigger cities could function at such a fast pace.

"No wonder so many people are unhappy," he mumbled to himself.

Taking another drink of coffee, the heat of it pricked something in his memory. As he was nudging it from his sub-conscious, the manager shouted, "Rooney! Get back out here.

This place is a madhouse. And no more talking. We have to get people through the lines."

As quickly as the thought troubled him, it disappeared as he chugged the rest of his coffee and tossed the Styrofoam cup into the trash can.

Maybe it'll come to me later, he mused as he walked out to greet the masses. His gut told him that whatever he was trying to remember was important, but it would have to wait.

CHAPTER TWENTY-FOUR

NADINE PUSHED OPEN the door of the sheriff station and walked inside, accompanied by a swirl of snow.

It had started snowing again, a prelude to the brutally cold night the meteorologists were predicting.

Joe and Eli were hunched over their desks, intently studying something that looked like a map of Saddle Hill.

"Hey guys," she greeted them. "I thought you could use a little pick-me-up." She held up a reusable shopping bag that contained hot chocolate and an assortment of muffins and scones.

Joe's weary face broke out into a smile as he stood to greet his wife. After dropping a short kiss on her head, he peeked in the bag.

"What did we do to deserve this?" Joe asked, taking the bag from Nadine's gloved hand.

"I know how hard you're working to find Marian, and I knew you wouldn't stop working to take a lunch break. I just want to make sure you're taken care of."

Joe smiled again. He'd told Nadine many times that her

nurturing spirit would make her a terrific mother. Now that she was only a few months away from her due date, it was obvious that her nurturing tendencies had kicked up a notch.

Unburdened from the weight of the hot chocolate and baked goods, Nadine stepped closer to Joe's desk. "Is that a map of Saddle Hill?"

"Sure is. We have a lead about where Marian might be."

Nadine's eyes widened. "Does this have anything to do with Henry Feinstein?" Nadine asked, studying the red outline around a property that looked to be on the outskirts of town.

"How did you know about that?" Joe snapped.

"Oh. Uh," Nadine stammered. "Holly mentioned that she'd heard something about Henry being a person of interest in Marian's disappearance."

Eli winced and looked at the floor.

Joe narrowed his eyes and glared at Eli. "Did you tell Holly we suspected that Henry Feinstein might be involved?"

Shifting from side to side, Eli admitted he did. "I just wanted to make sure she knew we were working on it and that there was hope that we might find Marian. You know how rough her life has been and how much she depends on Marian to be her family. I just wanted to help."

"You know we don't discuss ongoing investigations. What if the media got wind of the fact that you'd been out shooting your mouth off to your girlfriend about it?" Joe growled.

Eli ran his hand through already tousled hair. "I know I messed up. It won't happen again."

"See that it doesn't," Joe warned.

Nadine interrupted and pointed at the map. "What's with this property that you've got traced in red? Why is it important?"

Joe gave one final look of disapproval to Eli, whose face was still flushed with embarrassment, then walked back to his own desk to join his wife.

"That's a property that Henry Feinstein owns," Joe volunteered. "We haven't been out there to check it out yet, but according to the map, most of it is heavily wooded. We're checking with the utility company to see if there's water or electricity out there indicating that there might be a house on the property."

"Is there?" Nadine asked hopefully.

"Haven't heard yet. It's hard to get a response from anybody this close to Christmas."

Nadine twisted her hands together. "It's supposed to be so cold tonight, and we're supposed to get more snow and maybe some ice. I just can't stand the thought of Marian being out there somewhere, cold and alone."

"She might not be alone, Nay," Joe said, his face grim and his mouth tight.

Visibly shuddering, Nadine wrapped her arms around her belly and closed her eyes. "She has to be okay," she whispered more to herself than to her husband.

The room fell silent when the phone rang. Eli answered it with "Saddle Hill Sheriff Department, Deputy Eli Nolan speaking."

Joe and Nadine watched expectantly as Eli occasionally interjected things like "mmm-hmm" and "I see."

When he dropped the phone back into the cradle, he turned toward Joe and Nadine. "Good news and bad news."

"What's the good news?" Nadine asked.

"It seems that there is electricity running to the property, so if Marian is out there, it's possible that she's warm in some kind of shelter."

Joe folded his arms over his chest. "And the bad news?"

"It would seem that the electricity went out sometime last night and isn't expected to be back on for a couple more days."

"But it's supposed to be so cold tonight," Nadine protested. "She'll freeze to death if she's out there with no heat."

Joe studied his wife, who was blinking back tears. Marian meant so much to all of them and would be dubbed an honorary grandmother to his child. He couldn't let anything happen to her. Turning to face Eli, the young man's expression was the same as his own.

Jerking his head toward the door of the station, Joe said, "Let's go check it out."

"What about a warrant?"

"I'd say this is probable cause. The most important thing is that we find Marian. We'll deal with any backlash when it comes."

With a tight nod, Eli grabbed his coat and walked outside into the already blustery air.

"Be careful," Nadine whispered as Joe gave her hand a squeeze on his way out the door.

"I will. We'll find her," Joe promised as he followed Eli out to the car.

As she watched her husband drive away, Nadine silently prayed that they'd be safe out there, and that Marian would be found unharmed.

CHAPTER TWENTY-FIVE

PATRICIA JINGLE ADJUSTED and readjusted the stack of books sitting in front of her for the sixth time since she got to Dusty Jackets, Saddle Hill's local bookstore. It was the day of her first book signing, and the jitters had gotten the best of her. Though she knew people would be interested in learning more about her life behind the scenes as Mrs. Claus, she still felt nervous that nobody would show up to buy her book.

"Ready, Patty?" Johnny Palmer, the owner of Dusty Jackets asked.

Taking a deep, steadying breath, Patricia nodded and took her seat at the table behind the books. Against the backdrop of shelves lined with books, she finally felt like she was where she belonged. While she loved her husband deeply, she'd known for many years that she was destined for more than being Mrs. Claus.

An hour later, she'd only signed and sold three books, but had twice that many interesting conversations. It was a big day for her, and the excitement of it helped curb her worry about Marian. In fact, she noticed with a twinge of guilt that this was the first time she'd even thought of her friend since arriving at the bookstore nearly two hours earlier.

She hadn't heard anything about Marian's disappearance since this morning when she was at the Rose Petal Café with James and several others. Marian had been one of her closest friends for years, both sharing a special affinity for Christmas. Even though Marian thought the Jingle family went overboard in their year-long celebration of Christmas, she never said an unkind word about it, and even worked side-by-side with her oldest son, Kris, where he served as a mall Santa.

At the sound of the front door jingling as another customer entered Dusty Jackets, Patricia sat up straighter. Kris was walking toward her, a broad smile on his face. He stopped when he reached her and bent forward to drop a quick kiss on her cheek.

"Congratulations, Mom. I'm so proud of you," he said, his face glowing with joy.

"Thanks," she said, motherly love overwhelming her. He'd always been the black sheep of the family, resisting their treatment of Christmas. Despite that, he was a gentle and decent person with a good heart.

"How's it going here?" he asked.

Patricia shrugged. "I've only signed three copies, but I've talked to a few people who didn't buy a copy."

Kris picked up a copy of *Forever Mrs. Claus*, and held it out to his mother. "Make it four."

Patricia's smile lit up her round face as she took the book from her son's hand and scribbled a personalized greeting on the title page. Handing it back to him, she asked, "So where's this mystery girlfriend that keeps you so busy?"

A light blush crept up Kris's neck and onto his cheeks.

"She's not a mystery, Mom. And she doesn't keep me that busy. I've been studying for finals."

Kris, at the age of thirty-three, was fulfilling his dream of pursuing a degree in English Literature in hopes of one day teaching a college class on Shakespeare.

"If she's not a mystery, why haven't you introduced her to me and your father?" Patricia countered.

With a quick glance at his watch, Kris said, "She's actually supposed to meet me here now. She's interested in your book and hearing about what it would be like to live a year-round Christmas. I already told her what it was like from my perspective, but she pointed out that it was different because I didn't live at home with you and Dad anymore."

The mother and son looked up as the front door jingled open again. Patricia's heart sank when she saw that the reporter from WGNN, Carol Ling, was walking toward her, followed by a cameraman. It sank further when she watched Kris walk over to her and plant a firm kiss on her lips.

She plastered a smile on her face when he turned to finally introduce his girlfriend to her.

No wonder he'd kept her a secret.

In Patricia's opinion, this girl was only out to make a name for herself and would be intruding on everyone's lives until she got the story that would make that happen.

As the red light on the camera started flashing, an indication that she was being recorded, Patricia tried to focus on the bright side. As annoying and intrusive as she found Carol Ling, the free publicity might actually be a good thing. What harm could there possibly be in using it to sell a few books?

CHAPTER TWENTY-SIX

WINSTON MARSHALL TAPPED his pen impatiently on his desk. Until now, it had looked like this Christmas season was going to go off without a hitch. Here it was, three days before Christmas and his number one elf was missing and Kris Jingle, his last remaining Santa, had his head in the clouds most of the time. Rumor was he had a girlfriend that was keeping him preoccupied lately.

Never mind the fact that he'd gone most of the year without finding a suitable replacement for Joe Adler, who'd resigned his position as security guard to become the town's new sheriff. Since then, he'd been acting as security guard when something needed to be addressed, but running around putting out fires wasn't in his nature. He preferred to prevent the fires from starting in the first place.

Rolling his eyes and dropping his pen on the desk, he hoisted himself out of his chair and paced around the cramped office. Being the manager of a small-town mall wasn't the most glamorous job, he knew, but for him it was a chance to be in command of his own troops. The store owners and employees even called him "The General" behind his back as though it was some kind of mean nickname. The truth was, though, he loved it.

When his plans to have a career in the military went awry due to a heart murmur they'd detected during processing at boot camp, he'd returned to Saddle Hill feeling deflated and weak. A year later when the manager of the mall retired, he'd reluctantly followed his grandfather's advice and applied for the job. To his shock, he'd gotten the job and took command of his troops. But try as he might, he could never seem to make the place run like the well-oiled machine he knew it could. With a bunch of yahoos working at the stores, how could it?

At least they can all afford to pay their rent this year, though, he mused.

Last year several of the stores were on the verge of bankruptcy, including the most elegant in the Saddle Hill Mall, Stockton's Jewel Palace. A lucrative partnership with Sylvia Bell, a successful fashion designer and Saddle Hill's newest part-time resident, had put an end to Ralph's financial worries.

Winston's, too, for that matter.

Carla Whipple was able to keep her candle store, Whipple's Wicks, open thanks to her recent marriage to Ralph Stockton.

Winston stopped pacing and poured a cup of the coffee he'd made earlier that morning—decaf, just as his doctor had recommended—and walked back to his desk, plopped down in his chair, and pulled a small orange bottle from his desk drawer. Unscrewing the cap, he shook a small pill into his palm and tossed it in his mouth, then washed it down with the stale coffee, grimacing as it went down his throat.

The anxiety that came with the job was no picnic, but in his mind, it was a small price to pay. He closed his eyes and rested his head against the back of his chair as he waited for the calming effect of the medication to kick in.

It would be time to do a walk-through of the mall soon, and Winston was afraid he'd have to give the employees a kick in the pants to get their work done. He'd often heard that it wasn't his place to do it since they were actually the ones paying him to rent space in his mall, but what they didn't seem to understand is that by ensuring they're doing their job, he was helping them keep their stores open—not to mention the steady stream of income their rent payments produced for the mall.

Bunch of yahoos, he thought again as he opened his eyes, shook his head to clear his mind, and stood up ready to face whatever was about to come at him.

As he approached the door, a brisk knock nearly stopped him in his tracks. What now? he wondered.

"What is it?" he barked just before opening the door.

When the door swung open, he was standing in front of a woman with long black hair and almond-shaped eyes. Behind her was a man holding a camera. He'd heard there was a reporter running around town this week covering Saddle Hill's many Christmas festivities.

This is probably the mayor's doing, he thought. Becky Roswell wanted Saddle Hill to get the attention she believed it deserved. Never mind that boosting the local economy could mean another term in office for her.

"Can I help you?" Winston asked in a pleasant tone. There was no need to get on the mayor's bad side.

The woman smiled. "Yes. I'm Carol Ling from WGNN, *We're the Good News Network*, and I was wondering if you might have a few minutes to spare. I'd really love our audience to hear from one of the top business owners in Saddle Hill about your Christmas traditions here at the mall."

Winston smiled, his first genuine one of the season. This was just what the mall needed. With so many people shopping online and in bigger cities these days, this was his chance to tell the world that there were some experiences that just can't be replaced when you take your business away from local shops.

"Of course. I'd be happy to," Winston agreed.

Despite the trouble they'd been having in the Christmas cheer department with Marian missing and Kris off in dating la-la land, Winston had hoped that this reporter could help bring some cheer to him by raising awareness of the importance of shopping local.

For the time being, he would just push all the negativity out of his mind and be as jolly as old Saint Nick himself.

CHAPTER TWENTY-SEVEN

CAROL LING SMILED and held a microphone up to her mouth. Looking directly at the camera, she said, "Hello. I'm Carol Ling, here at the Saddle Hill Mall with the manager, Winston Marshall." She turned her attention toward Winston and said, "Mr. Marshall, you're a lifelong resident of Saddle Hill, and this mall has been the home of many of this town's wonderful Christmas traditions. I'm sure our viewers would love to hear about some of your favorites."

Winston cleared his throat and nodded while simultaneously tugging uncomfortably on the waist of his khaki pants. He'd have been happier if they were somewhere a little more spacious than his closet-sized office, but as his grandma used to say, *When opportunity comes knocking, it's best not to slam the door in its face.* "Of course, Ms. Ling. One of our biggest draws of the Christmas season is the annual Mountain Craft Festival, which brings artisans from as far away as five hundred miles. It's held each year the weekend after Thanksgiving and displays some of the best craftsmanship in the eastern United States."

From an oversized tote bag the cameraman had been

carrying, Carol pulled out a handcrafted wooden bowl and held it out in front of Winston. "I believe this bowl was sold at the craft festival this year."

Winston shrugged. "It's very possible. That would be just one example of the talent these artisans have. Everything from those wooden bowls, hand-woven baskets, quilts, and hand-dipped candles are available at the festival. Of course there's something for everyone. Candy makers even set up booths, which of course brings a thrill to the kids."

Carol nodded, her eyes shining with excitement. "This seems like a wonderful town for kids. Can you tell me about any other traditions this mall has that are geared specifically toward children?"

Now Winston really wished they were somewhere other than his drab, cheerless office. "Our biggest tradition is geared only toward children. In the center of the mall, which I'm sure you'll be able to get footage of, is Santa's Workshop. Each year from November first until the evening of December twenty-fourth, Santa and his merry little elf are ready and waiting to hear the wishes of our local children. It really is a special time…"

Winston wasn't sure if it was indigestion or some Christmas cheer, but his midsection suddenly felt warm. Was it possible that he was experiencing the joy of the season? As far as Winston was concerned, it was uncomfortable and he didn't know why anybody would want to feel like this on purpose.

Carol Ling's tone became more serious. "Speaking of Santa and his elf… is it true that Marian Bright, the beloved mall elf, has gone missing?"

"I… uh… I haven't seen her today. Th-that's all I can tell you," Winston stammered, the feeling of warmth in his midsection suddenly turning into a wave of nausea.

"Isn't it true that Ms. Bright actually went missing *last night* after an altercation during Christmas caroling?" Carol pushed.

"I wouldn't know, I wasn't there," Winston said, irritation growing. "What does this have to do with Christmas traditions at the mall?"

Carol shrugged. "Isn't Ms. Bright your number one elf? Shouldn't you be more worried about her?"

Winston cringed. This woman was going to make him sound like a cold-hearted Scrooge. "Of course I'm worried about Marian. She's been a friend for many years. I've been very busy today, and honestly, I haven't had time to think about much of anything other than running this place. Now, if you'll excuse me, I have work to do," he said, pulling the door to his office closed behind him and rushing down the corridor toward the shops.

"What about the Santa you employed that robbed Stockton's Jewel Palace last year?" the reporter called after him as he hurried away.

Winston could feel his face turning red as he fled, wondering if it was just his imagination or if this woman was dead set on pinning all of Saddle Hill's crime on him.

CHAPTER TWENTY-EIGHT

BECKY ROSWELL, THE mayor of Saddle Hill, twisted a lock of her shoulder-length, dark blond hair around her finger as she watched WGNN's interview with Winston Marshall.

"This is a disaster," she said, shaking her head as she watched Winston dart down the corridor away from Carol and the camera.

It had seemed like such a good idea to have news coverage of the town's Christmas festivities, but now Saddle Hill looked just as dysfunctional as the rest of the world. Instead of seeing a town that comes together to help each other, viewers would think the whole community was falling apart.

And what is Carol even doing covering the negative side of things? Becky fumed to herself. I called WGNN because of their reputation for reporting only on the *good* things that happen in the world. If I wanted all the terrible things to be dug up, I would have called any old news station.

She leaned back in her chair and released the strand of hair from her fingers, opting to chew on her lower lip as an outlet for her mounting anxiety. Looking around her office, she relished the rich mahogany furniture and the gas fireplace nestled in the center of the bookshelves opposite her desk. If things turned out as bad as she feared, this would be her only term in this office. Though she'd never set her sights on becoming a politician, Becky thoroughly enjoyed her role as mayor of Saddle Hill.

Unclenching her teeth from her lip, she sat up straighter. She took the role of mayor because she wanted to help the town she loved. Now, in the face of a kidnapping and terrible PR, it was high time she started acting like the mayor she set out to be.

CHAPTER TWENTY-NINE

"YOU WEREN'T KIDDING about being a good cook," Vito said, his mouth full of the potpie Marian had made for dinner.

"I'm so glad you're enjoying it," Marian said, glowing with pride. Since Holly had been spending most evenings with Eli the past several months, it had been a while since she'd been able to cook a big meal for someone. It was so good to see someone taking such pleasure in her work, even if it was her kidnapper.

Vito continued shoveling the food into his mouth like a man who hadn't eaten in days. "I haven't eaten like this since my mom died. My wife sure couldn't cook like this."

Marian jumped on the opportunity. "So tell me, what was she like?"

Vito's fork stopped mid-air. "Who? Mom or Sharon?"

"Sharon's your wife's name, I assume?"

With a gulp, Vito swallowed the food and took a swig of hot buttered rum. "Ex, but yeah. That's her name."

Sensing he wasn't quite ready to talk about his ex-wife, Marian stuck to safer territory. "Your mom. Tell me about her."

He wiped his face with his napkin and gave a little extra attention to his beard just under his lower lip. "Mom was great," he said, placing his fork in a small puddle of sauce on his plate. "Never met a stranger. She had this way about her that always put everyone at ease. We didn't have much, but she welcomed anyone and everyone into our home and shared whatever we had. Nobody ever went away from our house hungry. She taught us to take care of our neighbors and to respect the dignity of all humankind." Vito dropped his head. "She must be rolling over in her grave about what I've gotten myself into."

Feeling an unexpected wave of compassion for her abductor, Marian reached across the worn table for his hand and gave it a squeeze. "For what it's worth, you've been very respectful of me. You know, the kidnapping aside." Her attempt at humor was rewarded with a sad smile.

Marian released his hand and walked back to the stove and retrieved the carafe of hot buttered rum. "You look like you could use a little more."

As she refilled his mug, he said, "Apparently your recipe is pretty rare. Some cashier at the grocery store even recognized the ingredients as I was checking out. You didn't do that on purpose, did you?" Vito eyed her suspiciously, as if trying to figure out if Marian had been trying to pull a fast one on him.

"Don't be silly," Marian said, hoping her laugh didn't seem too nervous. "This is just the best way I've found to make hot buttered rum, especially around the holidays. The cinnamon sticks and dried cranberries really make it taste extra Christmassy, don't you think?"

"You know, you remind me of my mom," Vito said, his eyes looking a little glassy, proof that the rum was having its desired effect.

"Your mother sounds like a wonderful person, so I'll take that as a compliment," Marian said, mentally crossing her fingers that her captor would soon be loose-lipped enough to tell her why he'd taken her. "She must have been very proud of you."

Vito's head bobbed up and down. "She was. I was her baby. Can't say the same about my dad, though. Nothing I ever did was good enough for him." He paused and allowed a belch to escape before continuing. "'Vito,' he'd say, 'some days I wonder if you'll ever make anything of yourself.' I tried to make him proud, but I was always too soft for him."

Marian had a hard time believing the man in front of her had ever been accused of being "too soft." Gentle, yes. She could see that he had a tender streak. But *soft*? His rough and burly exterior looked anything but soft.

"Did Sharon agree with your dad?" Marian nudged, topping off his rum with more.

Eying her with an unsteady gaze, Vito snorted. "No. For her I was too unsophisticated. That's why she ran off to the city with some big-shot lawyer." He took another long swig of the rum. "You trying to get me drunk? Eh, doesn't matter anyway. I'd welcome it, actually."

Marian decided it was time. "Vito, you seem like a nice guy. How did you get wrapped up in kidnapping?"

With a hiccup, Vito said, "Business was bad. I needed money. Nobody wants to hire a handyman anymore. They just want the big, fancy renovation companies. Nobody fixes things up anymore. They 'renovate' them."

Marian nudged a little more. "But how do you even know somebody that would order a kidnapping?"

Vito shrugged. "I don't. I just replied to a letter I got in the mail."

"Who hired you to kidnap me, Vito?" Marian pressed.

"Don't know. Never met him. We only ever communicated with text messages. I don't know who hired me. I just needed money." With a final hiccup, Vito's head drooped forward, his bearded chin resting on his chest.

Marian leaned back in her chair and exhaled. She wouldn't get anything else out of him. Certainly not tonight, anyway.

Tapping an index finger on the rickety table, Marian decided her best chance of finding out who was behind her kidnapping was to find Vito's phone. As he snored softly across from her, she realized it might not be as easy as it sounded. This was a big old house, and he could have it stashed anywhere. She hadn't been allowed to roam through the house, so she wasn't familiar with the layout.

On the other hand, she thought, he doesn't seem like he's harboring a lot of secrets. He might have just left it out in the open.

Standing as quietly as she could so she didn't disturb him, she set off on her mission. This was her best chance to find out why she'd been chosen as the victim, and who was pulling the strings.

CHAPTER THIRTY

ONCE HOME FROM his long shift at the grocery store, Fred Rooney sat in front of the crackling fire in his living room and read the morning newspaper as his wife, Gert, worked earnestly on the sweater she was knitting for her miniature Yorkie. Unable to make sense of what he was reading, Fred dropped the paper to his lap. An encounter he'd had with that customer at the grocery store earlier in the day was still nagging at him.

"What's eating you?" Gert asked, briefly taking her eyes off the teal yarn.

Fred shrugged. "Just this customer that came into the store earlier today. I'd never seen him before."

"Why's that bothering you? You know we've had more visitors in town this Christmas season. The stories that came out about Saddle Hill after the robbery at Stockton's last year have increased our tourism all year."

"There was just something about him," Fred replied, shaking his head but never taking his eyes from the flames dancing in front of him. "He didn't look like he belonged here."

Gert pulled her eyes away from her knitting and studied her husband. "Now Fred, don't start acting like one of those old geezers who doesn't like anybody new coming to town. Visitors are helping to save our town. Local business owners are doing better than ever because of the tourists, and they're bringing with them new ideas about how to market to them. It's good for the economy."

"I guess," Fred grunted. "There's just something about him…"

A timer dinged, and, placing the half-finished dog sweater on the coffee table, Gert stood from her favorite chair and walked toward the kitchen where a pot of stew was bubbling away on the stove. Dishes clattered as she retrieved bowls from the cabinet and began ladling the stew into them.

Gert called Fred to the table, where he settled in front of a steaming bowl of stew and a plate of freshly baked biscuits. Usually his favorite winter meal, it did little to distract him from his ruminating.

She slid a mug of hot buttered rum in front of him and said, "You seem like you could use this tonight."

Fred stared at the steaming drink, then snapped to attention, his back straight and his head lifted. "That's it!"

"What is *it*?" Gert asked as she lowered herself into her own chair.

"Hot buttered rum! That guy I was telling you about. The one that bothered me. He was buying ingredients for hot buttered rum."

Gert picked up her spoon and began stirring her stew. "So? Lots of people drink hot buttered rum when the weather is like this."

Chewing his lip, Fred said, "But not like this. He was buying cinnamon sticks and dried cranberries for it."

"So?"

"So, there's only one person I've ever met that uses cinnamon sticks and dried cranberries in their hot buttered rum. Marian Bright."

"She had to have gotten the recipe from somewhere," Gert said, shrugging off Fred's concern. "It's likely that you just noticed it because Marian is on your mind. Don't make connections that aren't there."

"I guess…" Fred conceded, though a gnawing certainty in his gut assured him that a stranger in town who just *happened* to be buying ingredients for Marian's special recipe for hot buttered rum simply couldn't be a coincidence.

CHAPTER THIRTY-ONE

KRIS JINGLE CLEARED the dishes from the small table in his kitchen and plopped them into the sink. He knew he wasn't much of a cook but was thrilled to have the chance to finally have Carol over to his apartment. Since she was living in a hotel for the month, she seemed more than happy to accept the invitation.

"It was a lot of fun seeing Mom at the bookstore today," he said as he walked to the sofa and motioned for Carol to follow him. "She's always loved books, and it was really good to see her having a book signing for one she's actually written."

"I'm sure," Carol murmured as she settled in close to Kris on the sofa. "How about turning on the fireplace?"

Kris stood and walked over to his gas fireplace, where, when he flipped a switch, flames roared to life, licking the ceramic logs. He'd had the wood-burning one replaced last year and had never been happier than he was at this moment that he didn't have the hassle of lighting a fire with matches.

Carol rested her head on his shoulder when he sat back down. "That's better, don't you think?"

"Much." Kris reached over to flick the lamp switch off. The room darkened, now lit only by the glowing fire. "And that's even better."

A soft sigh was Carol's only response.

Twirling the end of her long black hair around his fingers, Kris asked, "I don't know what I ever did to deserve you, but whatever it was, I sure am glad I did it."

"Oh, please. It was my good luck that we bumped into each other in the parking lot outside the grocery store last month."

A small chuckle escaped Kris's throat. "Yeah, sorry about that. I'm afraid the insurance company didn't find our happy little accident as endearing as we did. I still haven't gotten my bumper fixed. Next time I'll watch where I'm going when I back out of a parking spot."

"I just wish I'd met you and come to this town sooner," Carol lamented. "It's so charming."

Kris turned to her, his eyes taking in her exquisite face. "Really? I mean, I just can't stop thinking you're way out of my league and that one day you'll realize it, too."

"Not a chance," Carol assured him, then became serious. "Tell me more about this lady that's missing—Marian Bright."

Kris released her hair and stared into the flames dancing in the fireplace. Releasing a lungful of air, he said, "Marian is one of the most beloved members of this town. She is always willing to help anyone in need and has truly never met a stranger. She was a teacher for forty years before retiring after her husband died a year and a half ago and has been a mall elf for the last seventeen Christmases. Everyone loves her. I've never met anyone that had something bad to say about Marian."

"It's just so awful that she's gone missing. Any idea what happened to her?"

Kris shook his head. "I don't think anybody does. It's almost like she just vanished."

"I heard her car was found outside that Feinstein man's house. I saw him yelling at her last night. She didn't seem worried, but I sure was nervous," Carol offered. "He seemed like he could blow at any moment."

Shrugging, Kris said, "I don't know much about him. He pretty much keeps to himself. His wife died several years ago, and since then, nobody has seen much of him. I think he's been in and out of jail a couple times for assault or something."

"Such a shame," Carol said sadly as she leaned deeper into Kris's side.

"It is, but let's not talk about him anymore. I have much more interesting company than Henry Feinstein." Kris pulled her close and buried his face in her hair. "You smell like coconuts," he whispered.

Pulling away slightly, Carol asked, "How is Nicholas doing?"

Kris dropped his arm from her shoulders and jerked away. That was one way to kill the mood. "I guess he's fine. I try to visit him at least once a month, even though he did his best to make sure I was the one sitting in that jail cell instead of him."

"Don't you feel bad for him?" Carol asked, her eyes wide with compassion. "He *is* your brother, after all."

Kris stood up and paced toward the living room window. As he watched the snow fall on the sidewalk below, he said, "He's in jail because he stole something. He stole something to frame me for it so I would go to jail. Not to mention all the grief he's given me over the years because I wasn't as Christmas-crazed as the rest of them. It's hard to feel bad for him after that," he snapped, not even trying to hide his frustration.

Carol joined him at the window and placed a hand on his arm. "I'm sorry. I didn't mean to upset you. I never had a sibling, so I don't know how this stuff works." She looped her arm through his and pulled him close. "Forgive me?"

He turned his head and looked at her hair shining in the glow from the fireplace and her slim figure with curves in all the right places. She was the most beautiful woman he'd ever seen, and she was with him. "How could I not?" Kris said, finally, though it really rubbed him the wrong way that she made him out to be the bad guy when his brother was clearly to blame for the rift between them.

"I hate that my introduction to Saddle Hill has been at a time when Marian has gone missing. I would have loved to have met her."

Kris turned to face Carol and pulled her against his chest. "You probably will. Within the next few days, if I had to guess. If there's one thing I know about Marian, it's that she won't let anything stop her from celebrating Christmas with the people she loves."

"Is that so?" Carol asked thoughtfully.

"Absolutely," Kris affirmed. "Besides, the sheriff's department won't rest until they bring her home. One of the deputies, Eli Nolan, has been seeing the young woman, Holly Berry, who's been living with Marian for the past year. From what I gather, he's pretty smitten with her and would do just about anything to make her happy. The thing that would make her happiest is to have Marian home by Christmas. My money's on Eli to deliver."

"Interesting…"

"Not interesting," Kris countered. "A man in love will do whatever he can to make his lady happy."

Carol raised her hand and checked her watch. "Oh goodness! The evening slipped away from me. I really need to get back to the hotel and get a little work done." She stood on her tiptoes and gave Kris a quick kiss on the cheek, then gathered her things and rushed out the door.

Stunned by her sudden departure, Kris watched through the window as she walked gingerly to her car, careful not to slip on the ice- and snow-covered sidewalk. He knew Eli would do anything he could to make Holly happy, because he was beginning to feel the same way about Carol.

Disappointment settled in his gut as he realized how eager she seemed to get out of there tonight.

What story could she possibly be working on that she had to rush off so fast?

CHAPTER THIRTY-TWO

"I WISH YOU'D have let me come to your book signing today, dear," James Jingle told his wife at the dinner table that evening. "I know you were nervous, but I wouldn't have done anything to make it worse."

Patricia put down the fork she was using to twirl her fettuccine. "I was nervous, but it really wasn't about that so much as I was afraid somebody would make a comment that would hurt your feelings. It's no secret that most of the town didn't exactly agree with our year-long Christmas celebrations. I didn't want you to get upset if that happened."

James reached over to his wife and grasped her hand in his. "I know our way of life has been ridiculed, but we've turned over a new leaf. I was the driver behind all the Christmas shenanigans, and I know there will be consequences because of it. There's no need to try to protect me."

Patricia gave her husband's hand a squeeze. "I like you better this way. Who would have ever thought it would be better to just live simply and quietly, blending in with every-one else?"

"Unless that wretched reporter has anything to say about it. I'm sure she'd be more than happy to bring attention to the life we're trying to leave behind," James grumbled as he released his wife's hand and picked up his fork, resuming his fettuccine twirling.

"You know, she seems perfectly nice," Patricia countered. "Nosy, but nice. The nosiness is probably part of the job. We all know it can sometimes be hard to leave work behind." She looked pointedly at her husband, who for forty years had been unable to shed his role as Santa Claus.

James snorted. "Well, I think it's impolite to be nosy, no matter the reason. She's a stranger to this town and has taken it upon herself to make all the problems everyone has known to the world."

Chuckling softly, Patricia said, "Well, I don't think her news station reaches the whole world." Her tone growing more serious, she added, "Also, she's bringing attention to Marian's disappearance, which is something we should appreciate instead of scorn. Marian is a friend to us all, and if Carol can bring it to the attention of someone who can help, that's a good thing."

"Whatever you say," James said, a noodle hanging from the corner of his mouth, sauce dripping onto his neatly trimmed white beard. When he had chewed and swallowed, he said, "How did Kris meet this girl, anyway?"

"He never said," she replied with a shrug. "I was thinking of inviting the two of them over for dinner tomorrow. What do you think?"

His mouth hanging slightly agape, James said, "A reporter? In this house? Do we have to?"

Patricia exhaled and pursed her lips. "You've got to stop

thinking of her only as a reporter, James. She's Kris's girlfriend, and from what I could see, he's quite smitten with her. We need to get to know her."

"Fine," the former Santa huffed.

"And you'll be on your best behavior, right?" Patricia gently scolded.

"I'll do my best. No promises, though."

"You know, Mr. Claus," she said, her eyes lit with laughter, "It would seem that jolly old Saint Nick is getting crotchety in his old age."

The corners of James's mouth drooped. "I'm not crotchety," he protested.

"Whatever you say, dear." Patricia wasn't about to let James's foul mood about their son's choice of love interest dampen her spirits. Her book was published, and though it wasn't selling many copies yet, her dream of being a published author had come true. On top of that, Kris had gotten serious with someone, and she couldn't help but hope that someday she'd have grandchildren.

No matter what James said, she was going to choose to be excited for Kris. The woman couldn't be nearly as bad as James thought. After all, her son was happier than she'd seen him in years.

How could someone capable of making Kris this happy not be a perfectly lovely person?

CHAPTER THIRTY-THREE

CLAD IN BLACK and pink pajamas, Carol curled her legs under her on the sofa in her room at the Saddle Hill Inn, her home away from home for the last four weeks, then opened her laptop. With a soft sigh, she smiled at her good fortune. Who would have ever thought a chance encounter at some hole-in-the-wall grocery store in a tiny town would have been such a stroke of luck? She'd never been so happy to have someone back into her car. The damage it sustained was more than worth it.

Kris Jingle would be good for her.

As she began tapping out her next story, her smile widened. Though she wasn't able to write about Marian's safe return home just yet, there were plenty of other notable things to write about.

Henry Feinstein's threats to a woman who disappeared just hours later, for one, she mused.

Good thing I have a face for the camera *and* can write a good story, Carol thought as her fingers continued to fly across the keyboard.

A little preliminary research showed that, just as Kris had said, Henry Feinstein had a police record that seemed to be growing by the year. It hadn't been hard to find the news stories about his various arrests. He'd yelled at Marian last night, and now she was missing and her car was found abandoned outside his house. Not exactly good news for WGNN, but a little more like the exciting and hard-hitting story she'd been eager to write.

Certain her boss would love it, she continued to dig up any and all information she could find on Henry Feinstein. The papers loved stories like this. Like a seasoned veteran, she wove together a narrative that was sure to turn the public's attention toward—and mold its opinion of—a man who seemed as good a suspect as any in Marian Bright's disappearance.

Her assignment of reporting the good things Saddle Hill had to offer and the various holiday festivities that made the town so enchanting would have to wait.

CHAPTER THIRTY-FOUR

December 23

MARIAN INHALED DEEPLY as she pulled a tray of Christmas cookies from the oven. Though the sun hadn't risen yet, she was wide awake and ready to do something that was certain to lift her Christmas spirit. Never one to feel sorry for herself for long, she'd woken up several times during the night with the unfamiliar ache of homesickness. The musty room she'd slept in smelled nothing like her usual holiday scent of pine and cinnamon, and the wind that howled all through the night wasn't combated by her flannel sheets and cozy down comforter. Instead, the windows of the drafty old farmhouse rattled with each gust and let in just enough below-freezing air to make her as miserable as she'd ever felt.

There was only one way to fight that misery: Christmas. Getting up early to bake Christmas cookies would do wonders for her and accomplish two things. Number one, she'd feel more like herself surrounded by the scent of goodies browning to perfection in the oven. Number two, the heat from the oven would help warm the drafty house.

When she pulled the last tray of cookies from the oven and slid them onto the ancient cooling racks she'd found tucked away in the bottom drawer of the oven, she turned back toward the refrigerator and began planning breakfast. Her kidnapper, who she now knew was named Vito, if he even woke up before lunch, would probably be battling quite a hangover and wouldn't want much. Considering all the hot buttered rum she practically forced down his throat, she didn't see how he'd have much of an appetite.

Not that getting him drunk had done any good. When she finally found his phone nestled between two sagging couch cushions, the battery had been dead. After spending another hour looking for the charger, she was finally able to access his emails and text messages.

What she found was a big, fat nothing.

The communication from the "boss" was as vague as Vito had said. There was no indication whatsoever about who was pulling the strings or why Marian had been targeted. For the time being, she was stuck here.

Grow where you're planted.

Roger's words reverberated in her mind. If she couldn't get away from this place, she'd have to make it somewhere she'd like to be.

Busying herself with breakfast, she clattered the pots and pans around, looking for a skillet to make scrambled eggs and sausage. With the smell of the hearty breakfast overpowering the scent of the sugar cookies cooling on the counter, she felt her spirits begin to lift.

A good meal always did that.

As she was scooping the eggs, sausage, and fried potatoes she'd made as an afterthought onto a plate, she heard the sound of shuffling feet behind her. Turning to face the source of the noise, her gaze met the bleary eyes of her captor.

"Good morning," she chirped cheerfully. "Sleep well?"

"I never sleep good in this rathole," he grumbled, his eyes scanning the kitchen and disappointment registering on his face. He clearly hadn't found what he was looking for. "You've been busy this morning," he observed.

Marian bobbed her head in agreement as she surveyed her morning's work. "I have. I was in the mood for Christmas cookies today, so I got up early to bake them. Then I thought it would be nice to have a good breakfast. Interested?"

"I could use something to eat. And coffee. Is there any coffee?"

"Not yet, but I'll start some." As she filled the reservoir in the coffee maker and scooped the ground beans into the filter, she mentioned to Vito that he didn't look so great this morning.

"Of course not. I drank too much last night," he said, then eyed Marian as she piled the food onto his plate. "I think you did that on purpose."

Marian blinked innocently at him and held the plate out for him to take. "Did what on purpose?"

"Give me too much to drink. You were trying to get me drunk," he accused as he accepted the heaping plate of food.

"I didn't exactly have a gun to your head. You could have stopped any time you wanted," Marian defended, "but I had a feeling you didn't want to stop."

Vito shoveled a forkful of scrambled eggs into his mouth and chewed thoughtfully for a minute. "So, did you find what you were looking for?"

Marian's smile fell. "What do you mean?"

"I'm no fool. If you wanted me out of the way, there had to be a reason. Did you find it?"

Marian grabbed a mug from the dish rack and poured a steaming cup of coffee, black, just how Vito liked it. "No, I didn't," she admitted, then slid into the chair across from him.

"Care to tell me what you were looking for?"

Marian shrugged. *Why not?* "I was looking at the messages on your phone to see if there was any indication of who might have hired you. There wasn't."

Vito swallowed the bite in his mouth and studied her. "I already told you that."

"I know, but let's face facts here. You kidnapped me. You drugged me and have been holding me hostage. I don't even know where I am. Let's be honest for a second. How could I believe you were telling me the truth when you did those things?"

Visibly wincing, Vito readily agreed. "That's fair. I know there's no way to convince you, but this isn't exactly something I enjoy doing." He took another bite. "Except your cooking. I have enjoyed that."

Marian smiled as she watched her kidnapper polish off the rest of his breakfast, then take a giant swig of coffee. "So what happens if you get caught?" she asked, her voice somber.

A shadow crossed Vito's face as he considered her question. "I guess I'll go to jail."

"That doesn't bother you?"

He shrugged. "Of course it bothers me. This isn't how I saw my life turning out. My dad always said I wouldn't amount to anything, and look at me. I'm living up to his standards. Or should I say *down* to them?"

Marian studied the man in front of her, a fresh wave of

compassion washing over her. Again, she realized that Vito wasn't a bad guy, just a guy who made a bad choice out of desperation.

Standing to take his plate over to the sink, he used his fork to spear the last few potatoes in the skillet, then retreated down the back hallway toward the bathroom.

Marian filled a mug with coffee and leaned back in her chair. Her appetite was gone.

It was just as well—Vito had eaten everything she cooked, anyway.

CHAPTER THIRTY-FIVE

NADINE ROLLED OVER in bed and looked through the frost-covered windows, illuminated by the streetlight outside the house she and Joe called home. It was cold out there, no doubt about it. In the distance, she could see snowdrifts piled around cars and mailboxes. On any other morning, it would have been a beautiful sight, a scene from a Christmas card. This morning, though, Nadine couldn't find the beauty in it.

"That wind was howling last night," Joe said, slipping his arm around Nadine, his voice still groggy from sleep.

"I know. I hope Marian is okay," she said, unable to keep her anxiety in check. "Where could she be? If she was wandering around confused somewhere last night, that would be a really, really bad thing. She couldn't have survived out there." She turned her face back toward the window, looking at the unforgiving conditions outside. Tears filled her eyes. Though she readily admitted that she cried much easier now that she was pregnant, she was certain that wasn't the reason she was now on the verge of a breakdown.

Joe's arm tightened around her. "I know you're worried

about Marian. We all are. Eli and I are doing all we can to find her. I promise."

"I know you are," Nadine whispered as a tear slipped down her cheek. "But what if you can't find her? What if no one ever finds her?"

A heavy sigh was his only response.

"Not that I doubt you," Nadine said hurriedly.

"I know," Joe mumbled, then sat up and flung the covers off. "You can't let yourself think like that, Nay. You'll drive yourself crazy."

"Where are you going?"

"To take a shower. I need to get out there and keep looking. We've got to lower your stress level. It's not good for the baby."

Before Nadine could respond, Joe was in the bathroom with the door closed. A squeak and low groan sounded from the bathroom.

"Everything okay?" Nadine called as she struggled to sit up and hoist herself out of bed.

"I think the pipes are frozen," he replied, his voice muffled behind the closed door. "I was too distracted to leave the water on a drip last night."

Her anxiety kicked up a notch, Nadine stuffed her already swollen feet into her slippers and rushed to the kitchen. When she tried to turn on the faucet, she was greeted with the same squeak and groan she'd heard from the bathroom only moments before.

With the subzero temperatures from the night before, pipes all over town would be frozen. A lot of them would bust, too. Today might be the day everyone had their own emergency and could only think about their own problems. They wouldn't be able to focus on anyone or anything else.

Nadine chewed on her thumbnail, a nervous habit Joe had been trying to get her to break since they went on their first date.

Was Marian okay? Was she warm enough? Will there still be enough people to look for her if everyone's pipes busted? The questions tumbled around Nadine's mind.

The question that nagged at her the most, though, was *Is there still even a need to look for Marian, or is it already too late?*

CHAPTER THIRTY-SIX

NESTLED UNDER HER plush down comforter but unable to fall back asleep, Sylvia Bell debated whether or not to call a friend. Right now, she needed to talk to someone, anyone, about the unshakable dread she felt. Her heat had gone on the skids sometime during the night, and as the temperature dropped inside her house, she was reminded that there was no guarantee Marian was in a warm, insulated place.

Glancing at the clock, Sylvia noted that it was only six o'clock in the morning. It would be rude to call someone this early, Sylvia reminded herself.

Unable to lie still any longer, she threw back the comforter, then immediately wrapped it around herself and stood up. Dragging it behind her as she walked across the bedroom floor and into the living room, she paused to check the thermostat. Fifty-five degrees. She blew a puff of air to check if she could see her breath. There was nothing. At least that's something, Sylvia thought wryly as she pulled the comforter tighter around herself.

Thankful that she'd had the foresight to keep an electric

heater in the coat closet, she shuffled toward it and wrestled the box into the middle of the living room floor. Once it was turned on high and the room began to warm up some, she decided that she couldn't wait any longer to talk to someone. She really wanted to call Nadine, but growing another human being was hard work and she needed all the rest she could get. Holly had still seemed miffed about Nadine chastising her yesterday on the drive to that old farmhouse and might not be in the mood to talk.

Biting her bottom lip, she decided to call Ralph and prayed Carla wouldn't be too upset about being woken up so early. Ralph, always there for a friend whenever they needed a shoulder to cry on or someone to just listen, would be more than happy to talk to her.

Padding across the floor to her bedroom, she retrieved her cell phone from her nightstand, unplugged it from the charger, and carried it back to the living room where she settled on the sofa directly in front of the heater. Selecting Ralph's number from her contact list, she waited while the phone rang and whispered, "Pick up, pick up," willing Ralph to answer.

A cheerful, "Good morning, Sylvia," greeted her from the other end of the line.

"Oh, thank goodness," Sylvia breathed in relief. "I'm so sorry to bother you this early, but I'm going crazy with worry about Marian and could really use a friend to talk to."

She could practically see Ralph nodding in agreement. He and Marian had been close friends for years, and Sylvia suddenly felt selfish for not checking on him sooner to see how he was holding up.

"I'm all ears," Ralph said, then added, "It feels so weird to know that someone I know, a *friend*, is missing. You see this kind of thing on the news all the time and are glad it hasn't happened to someone you care about, but how often do we really stop and consider the possibility that it *could*? I know I never have."

Feeling her stomach drop, she realized that Ralph was probably hurting more than he let on. Always the shoulder to cry on, she'd never considered that he needed support from his friends, too. "Are you doing okay, Ralph? I know you and Marian have been friends for a really long time. I can't imagine how hard this must be for you."

She heard him sigh, and realized she was right. Nobody probably had bothered to check on him.

"I'm okay, I guess. I realize there's probably nothing I can do, but I feel like I should be doing something. *Anything*. That maybe if I had been looking instead of being at the store worrying about what happened to her, maybe I would have been able to find her. I'm sure it's probably ridiculous to think that way, but don't we all feel a little bit responsible when something isn't going the way we think it should?"

Sylvia looked at the tabletop Christmas tree winking at her from the corner. "Yes, we do," she agreed, realizing that it had been bothering her more than she admitted that they hadn't been able to turn up a single clue about what happened to Marian when they were out looking yesterday. Ridiculous as it was, she felt like it was her responsibility to bring Marian home, too. Maybe they all felt that way.

"It was so cold last night," Ralph lamented. "I can only imagine what might have happened to her. I close my eyes and see her frozen to death on the side of some strange road." He paused. "Oh, that's terrible. I'm sorry I said that."

Doing her best to shake the image from her mind, she

reminded Ralph that if anyone was resourceful enough to find a way to survive the below-freezing temperatures, it was Marian.

"That's true," Ralph murmured, his tone cheerier than it had been when she called. "Part of the reason we love Marian is that she's spunky and always looks for a way to make things work out. Why didn't I think of that before?"

Sylvia's own spirit lifted, too. She hadn't considered it before, either.

"Listen," Ralph said, interrupting her thoughts. "I need to go. Our pipes froze overnight, and I need to try getting them to thaw before I head to work. The last thing we need is for them to bust."

"Okay. Thanks for talking to me."

"No problem. And thank you. I needed this," Ralph said just before the phone went silent in Sylvia's ear.

She placed her phone on the couch cushion next to her and stood, still wrapped in her comforter. Walking over to the front window, she noted that it had snowed even more during the night, and that a few flakes were still dropping from the sky.

Though the odds might be stacked against her, if anyone was a survivor, it was Marian.

Smiling faintly as she turned away from the window to check the water in the half bath beside her kitchen, she realized that the real magic of friendship was that sometimes, when you think you're the one that needs help, you reach out to someone and end up being able to help them instead. Sylvia, acting in fear and sadness, had found the strength to not only help a friend, but to help herself as well.

It was a strength she'd need to remind herself not to give up, that she had to keep searching for her missing friend.

CHAPTER THIRTY-SEVEN

HOLLY WOKE FROM a fitful sleep to the sound of wind howling outside her bedroom window. Clutching her flannel sheets against her chin, she replayed the nightmare she'd woken up from, drenched in sweat. She'd dreamed that Marian was wandering along the side of some dark street after running her car off the road, only to meet a deranged killer who had her tied up and was torturing her in a dark basement somewhere.

Groaning, she pushed herself up onto her elbows and looked around her bedroom. The first time she saw this room, it had felt like a warm hug from the quintessential grandmother, with the the pine furniture, flannel sheets, and hand-stitched quilt. Though the furniture was the same, she'd removed the quilt in favor of something softer and more modern. The sheets were still flannel, but no longer bore the red-and-green-plaid pattern that had been there before. Over the past year, as she became more and more certain that this was her home, she began putting her personal touches on the space. Now she wished she'd left it alone.

She also wished she'd accepted Eli's offer to sleep on the

couch last night. Despite her own desire to not have to be alone, she knew Eli needed to be rested in order to do his best work today. He wouldn't be able to get the sleep he needed if he was listening to her worry all night. That wouldn't help anything, and bringing Marian home was the biggest priority right now, not her desire to have company.

Stretching under the covers one last time before getting up for the day, Holly swung her legs over the side of the bed, slipped her feet into the fuzzy slippers Marian had gotten her for her birthday, and pulled on her flannel-lined, fleece robe, another gift from her surrogate grandmother.

After tying the belt around her slender waist, she shuffled down the hall to the bathroom, pausing briefly outside Marian's bedroom. Holly poked her head inside, hoping for a Christmas miracle but knowing there wasn't one. That was confirmed when she glanced around, noting that it looked exactly the same as it did last night, and yesterday morning, and the night before that.

Though it was decorated to Marian's taste, it held an abandoned look that was a testament to Marian's absence.

Fighting back tears and shaking her head against the fear that her nightmare might have been more of a premonition, Holly continued to the bathroom. She turned the handle on the faucet to splash her face with warm water, but none flowed. Frowning, she turned it off and tried again.

Again, there was nothing.

Another gust of wind outside reminded her that the temperatures had dropped significantly during the night, and that the pipes were probably frozen.

What do I do now? Holly wondered. Marian had always been the one to take care of things like that. It seemed like she always had an answer for everything, and somehow always got the problem solved.

If only Marian was here now.

Holly went back to her bedroom, picked up the phone and dialed the number she'd committed to memory. Eli would know what to do.

When he didn't answer, Holly decided that she was just as capable of solving problems as Marian and Eli. A few taps on the screen of her cell phone brought up a list of ways to deal with frozen pipes. She could take care of this, and when Marian got home, she'd be so proud of Holly for taking care of it on her own.

CHAPTER THIRTY-EIGHT

THE BACK OF Eli Nolan's truck slid as he pulled off the highway and into the gravel parking lot in front of the sheriff's station. Glad his grandfather had insisted that he invest in snow tires and a plow for the front of his truck, he'd been able to make it to work with minimal threat to life and limb.

He'd only lost focus for a second, and that was when his phone rang and he saw that Holly was calling. His immediate thought was that she might have heard from Marian, then convinced himself it was more likely that she was worried and wanted to find out if he knew anything yet.

Determining that it would be safer to let the call ring through to voicemail rather than answering on the treacherous roads, he let it go, promising himself he'd call her back as soon as he could.

He'd been disappointed last night when she told him she didn't need him to keep her company but was glad she felt secure enough to handle the night alone.

His lips twitched as a smile spread across his face. There was just something about Holly that screamed at him to help her. He'd only dated a few girls, but none of them could hold a candle to Holly. She was tough and vulnerable all at the same time, and he couldn't resist the combination. He knew about her police record, and though the lawman in him said he shouldn't be dating her, he knew she'd changed. He'd watched over the past year as she became more trusting and more joyful. He relished the smile he brought to her face and was proud that he was able to make that beautiful face light up.

Lost in his thoughts about Holly, Eli slipped on a patch of ice and nearly fell. Willing himself to get his head out of the clouds, he pushed the front door of the station open and was greeted by a rush of warm air and the smell of coffee brewing. All thoughts of returning Holly's call left his mind when he saw Joe already hunched over his desk.

"Looks like you've been here a while," he said as he slid off his coat and tossed it over the back of his chair.

Joe looked up to meet his partner's gaze. "Yeah, Nadine is worried sick this morning. Her mind keeps going to the worst possible scenario. Between you and me, I think losing the baby earlier this year made her more sensitive to losing people she loves."

Eli arched an eyebrow. "Seems to me it had the same effect on you. I've seen the way you worry about her."

Joe shrugged. "I guess so, but I don't think it's as general for me. I worry about Nadine and this baby. I don't want anything to happen to my wife and child. It's different. But for Nadine, I don't know if she'd be able to handle losing someone else she loves."

The two men were silent for a minute, then Eli tilted his head toward the papers Joe had spread out on his desk. "Whatcha got there?"

His attention back on his work, Joe explained, "These are the papers I'm trying to get together so the judge will give us a search warrant for Feinstein's property." He waved a hand toward the paper on the left of his desk. "This is the property map. I'm trying to figure out the best way to go in. There appears to be a little building in the middle of the wooded area, and I'm not sure which would be the best way to approach it."

Eli circled around the desk and bent over Joe's shoulder. "Looks like there's a creek on this side," he said, pointing to the bottom of the page, "and I'm guessing we shouldn't assume it's frozen over enough to cross. We should probably go in through this adjacent property." Eli's finger pointed to a plot of land at the top right of the page. "It will take a little longer, but seems the safest way in."

Joe considered Eli's suggestion for a moment before agreeing. "You're probably right. Now we have to wait and see if the judge thinks Feinstein's public threat against Marian, coupled with his arrest record and history of violence is enough for a warrant."

"Fingers crossed," Eli said as the phone on Joe's desk rang.

Listening as Joe interjected here and there as the caller allowed, he gathered that it had something to do with Henry Feinstein.

When Joe finally put the receiver back in the cradle, he confirmed Eli's hunch. "That was Feinstein's lawyer. Sounds like some sleazy ambulance chaser. Anyway, he's agreed to bring Henry in today so we can question him. If we're lucky, they'll give us permission to search the property and we won't even have to worry about a search warrant."

Eli slapped Joe on the shoulder in a good-job gesture, then

walked to his own desk. As he settled in, the phone rang again. This time, Joe put it on speaker.

"What now?" he heard Joe mutter as he greeted the caller.

Once the caller identified himself and told them the reason for the call, Eli's thoughts echoed what Joe had said.

What now?

CHAPTER THIRTY-NINE

FRED ROONEY WAITED as the phone rang, while his wife, Gert, looked on. She'd made it perfectly clear that she disagreed with his decision to alert the sheriff's office about the man who bought the same ingredients Marian used for her hot buttered rum.

"I have to tell them," he'd told her. "If I don't tell them and find out later that it could have helped bring her home, I'd never be able to forgive myself."

Gert had grumbled that he was going to look like a fool, and he would be taking up time that could be spent following actual leads.

Phone in hand, Fred was certain he was doing the right thing. In the twenty years they'd been married, there had been many arguments about things Fred and Gert didn't see eye to eye on. In nearly all of them, she'd told him he would look like a fool, and in nearly all of them, Fred went with his gut despite her warnings. Sometimes he looked like a fool, but most of the time he felt satisfied that he'd followed his instincts no matter the outcome.

Now was one of those times. No matter what people thought of him, he had to be able to live with himself.

When the sheriff answered, he rushed into his speech, giving his suspicions about the bearded man who came to the store buying Marian's one-of-a-kind, top-secret ingredients. A few minutes later, when he'd told all he knew, his hope dropped.

"How do you know he was making hot buttered rum with those ingredients? He could just like to drink rum, and was planning to make cranberry muffins," Joe countered. "My wife is quite a baker, and during the holidays, she uses those exact ingredients—minus the rum—in at least a half dozen recipes. I'm afraid there's nothing special about dried cranberries and cinnamon sticks this time of year."

"In all due respect, deputy," Fred argued, "Marian comes through my check-out line many times every holiday season. As you are probably already aware, she's a talker. She's told me more times than I can count about how she came up with the recipe after being at a Christmas party and deciding that regular buttered rum was too boring. Every year when I scan her items, I hear the story. That sort of thing tends to stick in a person's mind."

Gert's Yorkie sat at Fred's feet, giving him an accusatory look. He nudged it with his foot and it retreated to Gert's lap.

"Fred, I understand that you have spoken to Marian about the history of her hot buttered rum. Unfortunately, that's not enough to go on. I appreciate the information and it could be useful if we find evidence to support it. Until then, though, we have to move in a different direction," Eli interjected.

Fred frowned as the phone clicked in his ear, the dial tone humming an annoying cadence. He pulled the receiver away from his ear and scowled at it.

A satisfied smirk marred Gert's otherwise attractive face. "I tried to warn you. If you'd listened to me, you wouldn't have made yourself look like a fool in front of the sheriff and his deputy."

Fred narrowed his eyes at his wife. *I tried to warn you.* That was her version of "I told you so."

Dropping the phone back in its cradle, Fred knew in his gut that he was right and what he'd told Joe and Eli was important. Now he could only pray there would be evidence to support it so they would look into the bearded stranger who was making Marian's hot buttered rum.

CHAPTER FORTY

WIPING THE STEAM from the bathroom mirror, Vito Franks looked at himself as he trimmed his beard. Though his vision was hazy, he could still see how terrible he looked. The shower, though helping him feel cleaner, had done nothing to make him appear any less hungover. Mentally scolding himself for drinking so much last night, he realized that he wasn't sorry he did. The past few years had been so hard. Between Sharon leaving and taking the kids, his mom and dad dying, and losing his job, he was past due for a little overindulgence. For years he'd held it together, making the right choice no matter how tough things had been.

Until now.

One moment of panic had wrecked everything. All of a sudden, when he didn't have a job to go to anymore, but the bills were still coming, he knew he had to do something to make money. Then, out of nowhere, he'd been contacted to kidnap Marian Bright. The details were vague and the boss anonymous, but he'd had the impression no harm was supposed to come to her.

Or maybe that was just his own interpretation, and more orders would come later. Right now, he wasn't sure of anything.

The payment for the job was twenty-five thousand dollars. With that kind of money, he wouldn't have to worry about his bills for a while. One of the conditions was that he stay in this broken-down old farmhouse with Marian locked in the barn. That had seemed easy enough, and he'd planned to leave her alone in the barn. But here she was, puttering around in the kitchen making Christmas cookies and feeding him the kind of breakfast he hadn't had since he lived on his parents' farm.

He intended to keep his distance, to not get to know her. What he hadn't counted on was liking her so much.

How did I let it go this far? he wondered as he retrieved his straight razor from the rusty medicine cabinet above the toilet.

It had been a long time since his face had seen the sharp end of a razor, but it was time for a new start. That new start would begin with him shaving the beard he'd hidden behind most of his adult life. As the coarse hair fell into the sink, he imagined that he was shedding the part of himself that agreed to this terrible scheme right along with it.

Once he was finished, he examined his new look. He had a few nicks here and there but was satisfied with the overall result. Over the years, he'd forgotten what he looked like. Now, looking into the face with the dark eyes and strong, square jaw that had gotten him his fair share of female attention when he was younger, he realized he looked like he'd also shaved about ten years off his age.

Turning the knob on the faucet, he rinsed the sink, glad he had the foresight to wrap the pipes in the old house before the temperature dropped last night. Even though it wasn't the nicest place to be, at least he and Marian would have running water. It was something he guessed a lot of other folks probably wouldn't have today.

The clanging of pots in the kitchen reminded him that Christmas was only two days away and he had an unwilling houseguest.

What was she up to now?

Regret clenched his stomach. She didn't deserve to be stuck in this house for Christmas. Someone as loved as she seemed to be deserved to be home with people she cared about, celebrating the joy of the season.

Rubbing his smooth jawline, Vito recognized what he had to do. Even though he would be in trouble, he had to find a way to get Marian out of this house and back where she belonged.

CHAPTER FORTY-ONE

"SHE'S GOING TO be okay. I can feel it," Carla said, clasping Ralph's hand as he stared into his coffee cup, looking as deep in despair as she'd ever seen him. "Marian is a tough lady, and everyone in town is keeping an eye out for her. We'll get her back."

Ralph nodded absently, the drooping of his otherwise jolly face betraying his doubt that all would be well. "I'm trying to believe that. It's just hard to deal with the idea that she's alone and probably freezing when it's so close to Christmas. Thanks for the reminder, though, sweetie," he said, raising Carla's hand to his lips and placing a gentle kiss on her fingers. "Marian has been a friend for so many years, and the thought of her being out there in this…" he waved his hand toward the window that showed the snow was still steadily falling on their town. "I know she's tough, but she's still in her seventies. At some point a person's age has to be taken into account."

Carla squeezed his hand tighter. "What can I do? I know the sheriff's department is out looking, and I'm sure others are out looking on their own, but has anyone actually formed a search party? There are so many back roads on the outskirts of town, there's no way just a few people could cover the whole area."

Ralph raised his broad shoulders and let them drop. "Not that I've heard. I think Holly has been out looking some, but I don't know that for sure. She's probably completely heartsick. From the way Sylvia talked, I think she might be looking, but like you said, a few people can't cover the whole town, especially when you take the more rural areas into consideration."

Chewing her bottom lip in thoughtful silence, an idea formed in Carla's head. "I'll do it."

"Do what?"

"I'll take charge of forming a search party. She's been such a good friend to you, and she helped us find love again. Not to mention that she was the one that found out what happened to your Christmas star last year."

Tears welled in Ralph's eyes. They darted back to the window. "I don't know, Carla. It looks pretty treacherous out there. Maybe you shouldn't risk it. If anything happened to you… I just couldn't handle it."

With one final squeeze, Carla released Ralph's beefy hand and stood up with her shoulders back, determination written on her round face. Her voice resolved, she said, "I'm going to help find Marian. I can't just sit back and watch you worry. Besides, thinking about what Marian might be going through right now makes me feel sick. She's my friend, too, you know." Stooping over to plant a kiss on the top of Ralph's head, she added, "I'll be careful. I promise."

At that, Carla spun on her heel and marched toward the bedroom to get dressed for the day. Layers would be her friends out in this weather.

Now all she needed was a group of people who were also willing to risk their own safety for the sake of finding a woman that had brought so much joy to Saddle Hill.

CHAPTER FORTY-TWO

KRIS JINGLE SAT in Santa's Throne, scowling at the line of children. Unlike years before, his sour mood wasn't because of the kids and their endless Christmas lists. This time, it was because he couldn't shake the feeling that something had gone wrong in his relationship with Carol. He'd never had good luck with women, and since he'd met her, sometimes he had to remind himself that it didn't have to be too good to be true.

But maybe it was.

He knew Carol was way out of his league, with her good looks and a job that commanded respect. Never mind the confidence she exuded and the ease with which she took command of a situation. Compared to her, what was he? A part-time Santa who went to school and was one day hoping to teach English literature to a bunch of late teenagers and early twenty-somethings. It wasn't exactly a match made in heaven—at least not for her. He was in his thirties, balding, with a pale complexion that blushed too easily. Sometimes stumbling over his words, no one would ever mistake him for someone that had it all together. Carol, on the other hand, was everything a man could ever want. In his mind, he'd hit the jackpot.

The weight of a portly child climbing into his lap pulled him from his own thoughts and forced him to grunt. The boy tugged on Kris's beard and said, "Is this beard real?"

Moving quickly to untangle the chubby fingers from his hook-on beard, Kris finally managed a jolly laugh and asked in a voice heartier than he felt, "What can Santa do for you this Christmas?"

"Lots of things," the boy remarked as he pulled a wrinkled piece of paper from his pocket.

Kris groaned. "Here we go again," he muttered under his breath.

"What did you say, Santa?" the boy asked, innocent brown eyes looking into his.

"Oh, nothing. Tell me what I can do for you."

Successfully sidestepping the boy's question, Kris listened with genuine interest as the boy requested a long list of things, not for himself, but for friends and family and those that had less than he did. No wonder the Grinch's heart could grow three sizes because of unselfishness, Kris mused. He wasn't accustomed to the warmth that spread through his chest at this boy's selfless Christmas list. Flashbacks from Christmases past filled his memory. Kids smiling sweetly up at him while asking for the world, as if they had every right to claim each thing they requested.

Now, looking down at this boy with a heart for others, Kris had hope that miracles did still happen. Maybe one of those miracles would be for him and he'd be able to hang on to Carol, who suddenly seemed as chilly as last night's wind.

"Do you think you can do that Santa?" the boy asked when he was finished reciting his list of Christmas wishes.

"You know, son, sometimes Santa has a hard time remembering. Can I have that list so I remember exactly what's on it?" Kris requested, doing his best to sound as cheery as his dad did.

"Sure!" the boy agreed, happily relinquishing the paper into Kris's grasp. "Thank you, Santa. I want to do nice things for other people, but when you're a kid without any money, it's hard." Wrapping his arms around Kris's neck the boy whispered into his beard, "Thank you for helping me."

Returning the boy's embrace, Kris chuckled heartily. When the child finally let go, Kris scooted him off his lap in anticipation of the next kid in line.

As a little girl in pigtails made her approach, Kris stuffed the list into the pocket of his Santa suit, vowing to do whatever he could to make the generous boy's Christmas wish come true.

CHAPTER FORTY-THREE

WINSTON WATCHED THE scene unfold in front of him and smiled in spite of himself. Who would have ever thought that grumpy ol' Kris Jingle would actually be smiling at a child?

Proof that miracles never cease.

The problem was that Marian wasn't in Santa's workshop with him. Without her there, smiling at the children and handing out candy canes, it just seemed a little less festive. Never one to feel nostalgic or get choked up about sentimental things, seeing someone else in Marian's place still stung.

The mall employees often thought of him as ice cold with no heart. Raised by a military father who taught him that any display of emotion could also be viewed as a display of weakness, Winston couldn't let the mall employees know how much they meant to him. Fortunately, with everyone consistently showing up to work, he never had to face the prospect that he'd lose one of them.

With Marian missing and a less-than-jolly elf standing in her place next to an unusually happy Kris Jingle, he had to consider it a possibility that someone he cared about might be out of his life forever.

Feeling the unwanted emotions welling up inside him, Winston straightened his back and turned briskly on his heel, heading off in the opposite direction of Santa's workshop. There were more inspections to be made, and he couldn't stand there feeling sorry for himself or anyone else.

Just as he was leaving, the sight of a grown woman dropping into Santa's lap made him pause for a moment. Rolling his eyes at the inappropriate behavior and tempering his rising annoyance, Winston made the conscious choice to let it go.

He had bigger things to worry about, especially with an elf that looked as though she'd been sucking on lemons wishing the kids an unenthusiastic Merry Christmas then shooing them away.

"We've got to find Marian and bring her home," he muttered under his breath. "Wherever she is, we've got to get her back."

⌁

"You make a very handsome Santa," Carol crowed as she plopped into Kris's lap.

Heat crept up the back of Kris's neck. "What are you doing here," he whispered through a smile.

Carol smiled back and nuzzled into Kris's white hook-on beard. "To give you my Christmas list of course."

Over her shoulder, Kris could see Winston standing there with his arms crossed over his chest. Clearly Carol's appearance at Santa's Workshop wasn't something the General welcomed.

"What time do you get finished here?" Carol asked, pulling away slightly. "Because what I want for Christmas is dinner with you tonight."

Pulling the arm that was encircling Carol's waist toward him, he checked his watch. "I've still got a few more hours. Dinner tonight sounds perfect, though."

"Good." Carol stood and stooped over to drop a quick kiss on Kris's lips. "Call me when you're finished here."

Resisting the urge to wrap his arms around her and pull her in for a deeper kiss, he winked and promised he would. He watched Carol's back as she walked away, then looked back toward the line of children. Behind them, he could see Winston's lips moving. Who he was talking to, Kris didn't know, but whatever he was saying, he seemed angry and determined.

I hope it's nothing more than Winston just being Winston, Kris thought as the next child in line walked up to him and scooted onto his lap. Whatever was bothering him, though, seemed to be serious.

CHAPTER FORTY-FOUR

JOE AND ELI rolled their eyes and shook their heads as they listened to Fred Rooney describe the man who'd been in the store the day before buying ingredients for Marian's top-secret, one-of-a-kind hot buttered rum.

"You don't understand," Fred countered when they told him a drink recipe wasn't enough to go on. "Marian has come through my checkout lane dozens of times over the years, and every Christmas I hear her talk about her recipe and how she'd never had any quite like it. She's very proud of her addition of dried cranberries and cinnamon sticks to her rum. There's no way this guy would have known about her recipe unless she told him about it. I think he has Marian."

Joe bit his lip in an effort to keep himself from telling Fred that his theory was the most ridiculous thing he'd ever heard. Eli scratched his jawline where stubble had emerged from a few missed days of shaving. More patient and more willing to give people the benefit of the doubt than Joe, Eli said, "Now, Mr. Rooney. You have to admit that there's always a possibility that someone else had the same idea about making hot buttered rum that Marian did. Cranberries and cinnamon sticks aren't exactly unusual ingredients during the holiday season. Wouldn't you agree?"

"I guess so," Fred agreed after several seconds of silence. "I just don't see how it can be a coincidence, though."

Joe gave an encouraging nod to Eli as he continued, "It might not be a coincidence. Maybe this guy you're talking about does have her. But how do we find him? Do you know who he is? Do you know where he's staying? What about the car he's driving? Without this information, we have nothing to go on."

"But—" Fred began to argue but was cut off immediately.

"We appreciate your willingness to pass along this information," Joe said in an uncharacteristically gentle voice, "but until we can answer more of those questions, we are no closer to finding her than we were before." Joe thanked him, then pressed the button to end the call.

"I guess we should expect some wild theories," Eli said, leaning back in his chair and propping his feet up on the edge of Joe's desk.

With a scowl, Joe shoved Eli's still-damp boots to the floor and said, "Maybe it's not a wild theory. Maybe Fred Rooney is on to something. He's gotten to know most of the people in Saddle Hill through his checkout line. The problem is, we don't have any idea who this guy is or where he's staying. Even if he's our guy, without any more information we're no closer to finding Marian than we were last night."

As the two frowned and shook their heads at the frustration of not being able to find their friend, the phone rang again. "We need a switchboard operator," Joe huffed as he picked up the receiver. After an initial greeting, he listened to what the caller had to say before bidding them goodbye and hanging up.

"What's up?" Eli asked, leaning forward, his instinct telling him something was going on.

"That was Henry Feinstein's lawyer. He's bringing Henry by the station this morning to talk to us. Apparently he's got some stuff he wants to get off his chest."

"Good. Maybe we'll find out if he had anything to do with Marian's disappearance," Eli said hopefully.

Despite the hope in Eli's voice, Joe couldn't shake the feeling that if they didn't find something soon, Marian's time was going to run out.

CHAPTER FORTY-FIVE

MARIAN PUTTERED AROUND the old farmhouse, tidying and polishing things the best she could to pass the time. Vito had gone upstairs a couple hours before, and without having him as company, she stayed busy by trying to make the place look respectable.

The more she polished and rearranged things, the more she saw what a charming house it really was. Despite the musty old furnishings, in different circumstances, she could see herself being happy here.

At the sound of footsteps behind her, she straightened and turned around to face a freshly shaved man who bore little resemblance to the unkempt, rough-around-the-edges character she'd been getting to know.

"What happened to you?" Marian said, feeling how wide her eyes were but unable to make them go back to their normal size.

Vito rubbed his chin. "You like it? I thought it was time for a fresh start, and what better way to do that than start with a good shave?"

Setting the rag down that she was using to polish the nicked and scratched furniture, Marian placed her hands on her hips. "You look like a different person. I don't think I realized what a handsome young man you are."

A light shade of pink crept up Vito's neck. "It's been a long time since I've heard that. I've been hiding behind a beard for so long, I'd forgotten what I even look like without it."

Marian tilted her head and narrowed her eyes at Vito, a rush of motherly affection rippling through her. *Poor guy*, Marian thought. *It sounds like he's had such a rough go of it. First growing up with a father that belittled him, then having a wife that took up with some big-city lawyer, then losing his job. That's enough to drive anybody to desperation.*

Chewing the inside of her lip, a plan formed in her mind. Though she'd only known Vito for two days, their forced proximity to one another made it feel longer, and she'd developed an unexpected fondness for her kidnapper.

Oh gracious, Marian thought. *I've developed Stockholm Syndrome.*

Shaking the thought away, she wondered what she could do to brighten Christmas for him. He'd already made it clear that just having her company made it the best Christmas season he'd had in years. A fresh stab of compassion made her realize that she wanted to do more than just provide company. Though she hadn't had a choice in being here, she could make the choice to make this a wonderful Christmas for him even though she couldn't be at home with her loved ones.

Grow where you're planted. Roger's words again echoed in her mind. Considering the snow and blustery winds, Marian found it more than ironic that something Roger used to say in reference to gardening kept slamming into her mind.

"What? You look like you're up to something," Vito said warily, still rubbing his smooth face.

Marian could almost feel her eyes twinkle, a quality that made her a fantastic elf. "I'm just planning a little Christmas surprise, that's all."

Vito's mouth drooped. "You're not planning on running off, are you? Because that wouldn't be a good surprise. It might turn out to be a death sentence for both of us."

Rolling her eyes, Marian replied, "There's no need to be so dramatic. No, I'm not planning to run off. I do need to spend a little time in the barn, though."

Vito shook his head firmly. "No way. It's too cold out there for you to be hanging out in a drafty old barn. That's why I let you in the house in the first place. Besides, if I let you go out there, what's the guarantee that you won't try to get away?"

Marian felt the corner of her mouth droop. "I give you my word that I won't try to run away. I'm not stupid and I don't have a death wish. I don't know where I am, and look at the weather. I'd freeze to death out there. If it makes you feel any better, you can come with me and keep an eye on me the whole time," she urged.

Vito frowned. "But it's freezing out there."

"I know," Marian said, holding her breath and hoping Vito would agree to let her.

Several beats passed before Vito finally agreed. "Fine. But I'll have to keep you in my sight. Consider it health insurance for both of us."

"Agreed," Marian sighed, her hope soaring. She'd be able to do something to let Vito know he mattered to somebody. That's what he really needed this Christmas: to know somebody cares.

"Let me go change." Vito's eyes scanned the clothes Marian had been wearing for the past two days. The pants had spots of food on them and the Christmas sweater, complete with colorful puff balls hanging loosely from the boughs of a Christmas tree, was rumpled from being slept in. "I'll see if I have something warmer you could wear."

As Vito walked from the living room in the direction of his bedroom, Marian reminded herself that Vito seemed to have a good heart, kidnapping aside. He was just a man that had hit hard times and made a bad choice because of it. Her gut told her he'd never hurt her.

"Try this on," he said when he returned a couple minutes later. He was holding a thick flannel shirt and wool socks. "I'm afraid those pants will have to do," he said, nodding toward her stained ones.

Marian slipped the flannel shirt on over her sweater and the socks over her own, tucking the legs of her pants into them. With the shirt falling to just above her knees and her hands lost inside the sleeves, she felt the way she did when she used to put on her dad's flannel shirts as a kid. He'd laughed at her and said she'd have some growing to do if she ever wanted to fill them out.

An amused smile dancing on Vito's face, he said, "Looks like I'm a little bigger than you. At least it will help keep you warm… at least down to your knees."

Stuffing her feet into the snow boots she'd worn Christmas caroling two days before and pulling on her winter coat, she hoped she'd find something in the barn she could use. As the two trudged through the snow, Marian relished the fresh air whipping against her face. This was the first time she'd been out of the house in two days, and even though it was well below freezing, she vowed to soak up as much of the cold, clean air that she could before she was shut away again.

As they walked toward the barn, she began singing "I'll Home for Christmas," and was surprised when Vito completed the line in a clear tenor voice. "… if only in my dreams."

A dull ache settled in Marian's midsection.

Right now, being home for Christmas really did seem like it would only happen in her dreams.

CHAPTER FORTY-SIX

IN THE CENTER of Whipple's Wicks, a small group of people gathered, murmuring to one another excitedly as Carla rang up the final customer before she closed the shop.

Thanks to an email blast she'd sent to everyone she knew, the search party Carla had vowed to assemble had shown up, and they were all eager to get started in their search for everyone's favorite Saddle Hill citizen.

Quickly ushering the straggling customer out of the store with a cheerful, though rushed, "Merry Christmas," Carla flipped the sign on the door over to say "Closed" and locked the door so no one else could come in.

With a sigh, she turned toward the group and said, "I'm so glad you all could be here. Marian has been a friend to us all, and now she needs our help. She's always been there for us when we needed her, now we have the opportunity to repay the favor. Though our very capable sheriff's department is looking for her, there are just too many remote places in Saddle Hill for them to cover by themselves. With all of us working together, I'm sure we can have her home for Christmas."

"But how will we know where to start?" a voice chimed out from the middle of the crowd. All heads turned toward the man who was speaking.

"Winston!" Carla gasped. "I'm so glad you could make it." He was the last person she expected to see and had second thoughts about even sending the email to him. Not known for displaying any sort of warmth to others, she couldn't believe he'd actually show up to help find Marian, especially during business hours. She didn't think he cared about anything other than the almighty dollar. Carla gave herself a mental shake. Everyone loved Marian, and that included Winston Marshall. As tough as he tried to appear, even he couldn't help but like Marian.

Sylvia Bell flashed a quick smile at Winston, then, emerging from the group, replied, "I think we can all agree that no stone should be left unturned in our search for Marian. Carla has called us together because as a group, we're stronger than we are as individuals. Instead of feeling overwhelmed, let's listen to Carla and hear what she has to say."

Carla shot Sylvia a grateful look and cleared her throat. "While it's true that there are a lot of out-of-the-way places in our town, who better to look in those places than people who live here. Looking around the group, I see several of you that live in the more rural areas of Saddle Hill. Those are just the people we need searching the more remote areas." Glancing around the search party, Carla pointed toward three people standing around the edge of the group. "I know you guys live farther out. You'll be one group, and I'll have you search the areas at the north side of Saddle Hill that aren't as familiar to those of us who live closer to town."

Carla was rewarded with a nod of agreement from the trio, who then turned to leave.

"Please contact me or the sheriff's department if you find anything," she called after them as they flipped the lock and walked out of the store. Turning her attention back to the group, she said, "We'll need a few more people to check the more wooded areas on the east side."

Sylvia raised her hand. "Holly, Nadine, and I have already been through there, but couldn't do a thorough check. I'd be more than happy to go again," she volunteered.

"Sounds good. Take Holly with you, but I'd be too worried to send Nadine out there. Make sure you have snow tires, and don't forget to pack food, water, and blankets just in case you get stuck out there," Carla suggested, as she set about the task of splitting the rest of the search party into smaller groups.

Within twenty minutes, everyone knew where they were supposed to be looking. Feeling satisfied that she was actually doing something to help bring Marian home, Carla inhaled the seasonal fragrances filling her candle shop. As she looked at the candles filling the shelves, she had an inspiration for a new Christmas scent. In honor of Marian, it would be scented with cranberry, orange, and cinnamon with just a hint of rum.

The name of the candle would be "Home For Christmas."

CHAPTER FORTY-SEVEN

ACCOMPANIED BY HIS lawyer, Henry Feinstein sat at the table in the interrogation room at the sheriff's station.

"So, Feinstein, are you here to confess to doing something to Marian Bright?" Joe asked, a hard edge to his voice.

Henry Feinstein started to object, but his lawyer, a small man with round glasses and a receding hairline, cut him off. "Let me begin by saying that we're here against my recommendation. I don't believe anything good will come from Henry speaking to you, but he insists."

"Maybe he's smarter than he looks," Joe muttered under his breath.

Eli shot Joe a disapproving look, then said, "We're glad you're here, Mr. Feinstein, and we're very interested in hearing what you have to say."

A wary look on his face, Henry cleared his throat and began, "First of all, I want to say I don't have anything to hide. I admit my past is a bit… checkered, but I wouldn't hurt anybody."

Eli shuffled through a small stack of papers on the table in front of him. "That's odd, considering that one of your arrests was because you assaulted someone."

Henry splayed his hands in front of himself and protested, "I'd never do that if I was in my right mind. That was the bottle."

"I suppose the bottle just jumped into your hand and the booze forced its way down your throat." Sarcasm dripped from Joe's voice.

Henry's head dropped, shame on his face. "I haven't felt like myself since my wife died. It hurt so much, I just had to make it stop. That's when I started drowning my sorrows."

"I'd like to point out that this line of questioning has nothing to do with what you suspect my client of doing," the lawyer said, pushing his glasses up the bridge of his nose. "If this doesn't become more relevant, I'm afraid I'll have to insist that my client cease answering any more of your ridiculous questions."

"Have it your way," Eli said. His tone softened and he continued in a different direction. "Tell me about Marian Bright."

Henry shrugged. "What about her?"

Joe flicked his eyes toward the lawyer and rolled them. He opened his mouth to talk, but Eli hurried on with his questions.

"You had some pretty strong words for her the other night when she was caroling at your house. Several people heard you make threats against her, including me," Eli reminded him.

Henry rubbed the stubble on his face. "That was the whiskey talking. Marian has always been good to me. She, along with her late husband, helped me a lot when my wife died."

Eli nodded, brought his fingers to a point under his chin, then said, "We've got proof that you have property way out on the outskirts of town, most of which is heavily wooded. That would be a good place to hide somebody you've kidnapped. We also happen to know there's a small building on that property. Care to tell us about that?"

"Whoa, whoa, whoa!" Henry bellowed, holding his hands out in front of himself as though shielding an attack. "Yes, I have property. It had been in my wife's family for generations. Her grandparents were farmers, but her parents weren't much into living off the land. Neither was she. It passed to me when she died, and I've never had any use for it. I can't grow a darn thing, and can't tell the difference between a cow's udder and a bull's… well, you get the idea. I ain't a farmer, either."

Joe chuckled while Eli cocked an eyebrow. The lawyer exhaled and rubbed his face, possibly realizing it was hopeless to try to get his client to stop talking.

After a moment, Joe said, "Let's talk about the night you threatened Marian, which coincidentally is the same night she disappeared. We found her car on the street across from your house, by the way."

"That is a coincidence," Henry said. "I can promise you that."

"Is that so?" Joe challenged. "Unfortunately for you, your word doesn't hold that much weight around here."

Pausing to glance at his lawyer, Henry looked as though, for the first time, he cared about his counsel's advice. After a single nod from the bespectacled attorney, Henry looked back at Joe and Eli. "I have proof."

"And what kind of proof might that be?"

The answer came after Henry took another quick glance at his attorney. "I have security cameras all around my house. If you want proof that I didn't have anything to do with Marian's disappearance, watch the camera footage. If she came into harm's way in front of my house, the cameras will show you that I had nothing to do with it."

Joe and Eli exchanged glances, knowing they were both having the same thought.

Now what?

Without Henry as a suspect, they were back to square zero.

Against their better judgment, they'd hung all their hopes of finding Marian on Henry Feinstein. If the cameras showed what Henry said they would, Feinstein would be off the hook. All they could do was pray that the time they wasted focusing on him wouldn't mean that it was too late to find Marian alive and well.

CHAPTER FORTY-EIGHT

KRIS JINGLE PUSHED the shopping cart around the Saddle Hill Market. Just as he'd promised the boy from that morning, he would fulfill the Christmas list that was full of gifts for other people.

Now, this is a kid that understood the true meaning of Christmas, Kris thought as he dropped several sticks of deodorant and bottles of shampoo into the cart. At the top of the list was toiletries and coats for the few homeless folks that resided in Saddle Hill. Once he got the toiletries and went back to the mall to pick up some winter coats to drop by the shelter, he'd tackle the next item on his list.

The boy's teacher was recipient number two. According to the good-hearted little boy, his teacher's husband had recently gotten injured at work and was unable to hang onto his job. The boy just wanted to make sure his teacher and her family had a nice Christmas dinner. Kris was sure Nadine, community spirited as she was, would gladly cater a Christmas feast for the family to remember. Along with the meal, he'd supply them with a gift card to the grocery store and a few toys for the teacher's kids.

The last item listed was something for the sheriff. The boy said that even though Saddle Hill doesn't have much crime, the sheriff still works really hard to make sure everyone is safe. Kris couldn't help but smile as he imagined grumpy Joe Adler getting a gift from a small boy in town that he probably didn't even know. This gift would take more thought, and Kris had to make sure it was a good one.

Feeling a bit guilty for missing the gathering of the newly formed search party, Kris reminded himself that what he was doing was something that would make Marian proud. Always ready to help others, he knew in his gut that Marian would approve of what he was doing.

There were plenty of people to look for her, but he was the only Santa that had been entrusted with the responsibility of fulfilling a selfless boy's Christmas wish list. For the first time in his life, Kris felt like he was being true to his role as Santa. The corner of his mouth twitched.

Dad would be proud.

CHAPTER FORTY-NINE

BUMPS AND CRASHES came from the barn as Marian dug through the piles of old farming tools and equipment.

"What exactly are you looking for?" Vito asked, his hands thrust deep into the pockets of his coat. A small cloud floated in front of his face as he spoke.

Marian stood as she examined a rusty old tiller blade. "I'll know it when I see it," she said absently, laying down the blade and getting back to her mission.

"How long will you be?" Vito urged. "It's cold out here." He glanced toward the pile of hay where he'd put Marian after kidnapping her and wondered how she didn't freeze to death that first night.

"It'll take as long as it takes. Don't rush me," Marian gently scolded.

"Can't you think of a better way to use your time instead of standing out here freezing?" Vito grumbled.

Marian turned to face him and placed her hands on her hips. "Nobody said you have to be here. You are more than welcome to go inside."

"You know I can't do that," he huffed, then walked over to the corner where a bale of hay lay against the wall. "I have to keep an eye on you. Make sure you don't try to run off."

Marian waved a gloved hand toward the frosted window. The snow lay thick on the ground and there was nothing—and no one—to be seen. "Do you really think I'm that stupid? I'd freeze to death out there. I wouldn't even know which direction to go to find my way back to town." The corner of her mouth drooped. "I was unconscious when you brought me here. Remember?"

Vito looked as though he was considering what she'd said, but he didn't budge from his spot on the hay bale. Marian shrugged and went back to her task. Within a few minutes, movement from the corner of the barn caught her attention. Vito was now standing and making his way to the door.

"Make sure you come straight back to the house when you're finished whatever it is you're doing," he ordered. "And don't take too long."

"Yes, warden," Marian said with a smirk and continued rummaging.

Raising her head and looking out the window, she watched Vito hike through the snow back to the farmhouse. As he ascended the steps onto the wide front porch, she breathed a sigh of relief. "Finally."

Ignoring the numbness creeping into her fingers, Marian continued her search.

"Bingo!" she exclaimed when she came upon a tractor seat. The cover was torn and falling apart, but there had to be something she could do to turn it into something better. "Upcycling" she thought it was called these days.

She gently laid it to the side as she continued searching.

An idea popping into her mind, she retrieved the tiller blade she'd discarded and put it with the tractor seat. More digging led her to more finds, and Marian was certain she'd be able to make something truly spectacular that would bring a smile to Vito's face.

Tonight, after he went to bed, she'd get started on her projects. Carefully hoisting the items into her arms, she kicked the barn door open, then shut it behind her as she labored under her load through the snow back to the house.

The sun was beginning to set, and a pang of homesickness twisted in Marian's stomach. This wasn't how she envisioned spending the last few days before Christmas, but here she was. Might as well make the best of it, she thought, still hoping against hope that she'd wake up Christmas morning in her own bed. Until then, though, she was going to tap into her inner elf and make it a Christmas to remember for her down-on-his-luck captor.

CHAPTER FIFTY

BEFORE SYLVIA STOPPED by Stockton's Jewel Palace to collect Holly for their foray out into the woods, she stopped by the Rose Petal Café for a muffin and a cup of coffee. Remembering what Carla had said about water and food, she ordered a few extra goodies and a few bottles of water. A stop by one of the department stores to pick up some blankets might be in order too, she reminded herself.

An exhausted-looking Nadine emerged from the kitchen just as Sylvia was paying. She eyed Sylvia's order suspiciously and asked, "What's up? No diet today?"

Sylvia flashed a smile, revealing a row of perfect teeth. She knew other women often envied her appearance, and she realized that Nadine was probably longing for her slim figure to return. Being in fashion and always feeling like she had to watch her weight was a burden. Everyone always expected her to look just right, and while she enjoyed looking good in her clothes, sometimes she just wanted to be able to let it all go. "In case I have a hunger emergency."

"A hunger emergency? Your house is close enough to town

that even a city driver like you should be able to make it to a store or restaurant without issue." Humor danced in Nadine's eyes, briefly erasing the dark circles under them.

"Will there ever be a day when I won't be viewed as a 'city girl?'" Sylvia said, exhaling in mock exasperation.

"Spend more time here and we'll see." Nadine nodded toward the bag of pastries Sylvia had just bought. "What's really going on?"

Tightening her hand around the top of the bag, Sylvia told her about the search group Carla had organized. "Holly and I are going back out to look for Marian. Carla suggested we take food and water."

"If you'll wait a minute, I'll come with you. I just need to make sure everything is under control here," Nadine said as she turned back toward the kitchen.

A knot settled in Sylvia's stomach. "I don't think that's such a good idea," she said, then knew from the look on Nadine's face that she was having the exact reaction Sylvia feared she would.

"What do you mean it's not a good idea?" Nadine challenged. "It was a fine idea yesterday when we were out looking for her. What changed?" She raised her chin a fraction, an unconscious move that reminded others that even though Nadine was sweet and wouldn't hurt a flea, she wasn't one to back down from what she thought was right.

"The road conditions are what changed, and it probably wasn't wise to have you out on the slick roads yesterday, either," Sylvia said, mentally pleading that Nadine would understand this was for her own safety. "It's not safe for you out there."

Nadine's head jerked back as though she'd been slapped.

"It's not safe for you either, but you're still going. Marian is my friend, too. I want to help."

Sylvia took a steadying breath, hoping she could find the right words and not upset Nadine even more. She gestured toward Nadine's round stomach. "There's more risk for you. If something happened to you and that little guy, I'd never be able to forgive myself. Joe would never forgive me, either. I need you and that baby to be okay so I can look at myself in the mirror and not feel like I ruined lives." Sylvia forced a smile. "Also, I want to be an honorary aunt to that little guy."

Nadine's eyes softened slightly, then dropped to her belly. "Joe has been so worried that something would go wrong. He treats me as though I'm this fragile creature that might break if anything so much as brushes up against me. Deep down, I wonder if he thinks the miscarriage was my fault."

Sylvia placed the bag on the counter and stepped closer to her friend, wrapping her arms around Nadine's shoulders. "I'm sure he doesn't think that. He worries about you because he loves you, and he loves the little human growing inside you. I'm sure he doesn't blame you for the miscarriage. These things happen all the time. But I do know he would blame *me* if I let you go with me and something happened to you. I couldn't live with being responsible for hurting you."

Tears sprang to Nadine's eyes, and Sylvia reached over to the napkin dispenser on the counter, pulled one out, and handed it to her friend. "I'm so tired of feeling useless. I'm tired of not being able to live my life without worrying that I'm putting someone else's in danger." The circles under Nadine's eyes darkened. "I'm just tired."

Sylvia held her friend tighter. "I know, sweetie. I'm sure it's not easy to give yourself up so completely for someone else, but when it's your unborn child, it's the right thing to do. I'll tell you what. When Marian gets home, you can be in charge of cooking enough to feed her for a week." Sylvia loosened the embrace and put her hands on Nadine's shoulders. She looked into her friend's eyes and said firmly, "You are *not* useless."

Nadine sniffed and pulled away from Sylvia. "You're right. Of course, you're right. Go find Marian."

Sylvia wiped a tear from Nadine's cheek and gave a subtle nod, picked up her bag of pastries, then went off to buy a few blankets.

Fifteen minutes later, armed with bags bulging with supplies, Sylvia walked into Stockton's Jewel Palace and brought Holly up to speed on the search party and their assignment.

"What's with the shopping trip?" Holly asked, cocking her head toward Sylvia's purchases.

"Carla said we should have food, water, and blankets in the car just in case we got stuck somewhere, so I bought food, water, and blankets. We're all set. Let's go," Sylvia urged.

Holly nodded. "I need to let Ralph know I'm leaving. It shouldn't be a problem since hardly anyone has been in all day. Last-minute shoppers don't tend to shop for diamonds." She disappeared into a room in the back, then emerged a few minutes later. When she returned, she picked up one of the bags Sylvia had deposited on the floor and the two women fell into step with each other.

"Let's pray we don't need these," Sylvia said, slightly raising the bags she was holding.

"No kidding. Are we stopping by the café to get Nadine on our way out?"

Sylvia shook her head tightly. "We can't risk anything

happening to her or the baby out on these roads. From what I hear, they're pretty treacherous, especially out on the edge of town."

"I bet she's pretty upset about having to sit this one out," Holly observed, knowing Nadine was having a tough time with the limitations that came with pregnancy.

"More than upset, but she knows staying here is the right thing to do. We've got to help keep her safe."

Holly agreed, but the tension on her face communicated that she was also more than a little worried about their own safety.

The two walked out of the mall and crossed the slippery parking lot, dropped the food and blankets in the backseat, and slid into the car.

Sensing Holly's discomfort, Sylvia reached across the center console of her car and squeezed Holly's hand. "For Marian."

"For Marian," Holly repeated, her voice determined. "Let's go bring her home."

CHAPTER FIFTY-ONE

ELI WALKED THROUGH the squad room toward his desk, passing Joe's desk on his way. Noticing his partner's concentration on his computer screen, he stopped. "What's that?"

Never taking his eyes from the screen, Joe said, "Feinstein's lawyer sent the video footage over from his security cameras."

Leaning over Joe's shoulder, Eli watched as snowflakes fell. "Looks pretty peaceful," he observed.

"Too peaceful," Joe agreed. "Henry really needs us to find something on these videos to clear his name. Otherwise, he's still suspect numero uno."

"You mean suspect numero *only*," Eli said, then straightened back to a standing position. "I just got off the phone with Holly. Apparently Carla organized a search party and is sending people all over town looking for Marian."

Heat crept up Joe's neck and turned his face crimson. "That's not her place," he snapped.

"Maybe not, but we certainly could use the help," Eli said with a shrug. "The two of us can't look everywhere for her."

"Still," Joe huffed. "She should have asked us first. We

could have organized it better and sent them to locations where it's most likely that someone could be keeping her."

"Perhaps," Eli acknowledged, "but it's too much for the two of us. We need help. You know that, whether you want to admit it or not."

Joe's stubborn streak and his propensity to follow the law to the letter was well-known. His ability to go with the flow and change directions mid-course wasn't.

Chewing on his lip, Joe seemed to be considering Eli's point. "I guess it won't do any harm. I just hope nobody gets hurt traipsing around chasing wild geese."

Eli cocked an eyebrow at Joe. "It's not a wild goose chase, Joe. We know Marian has to be out there somewhere, and until we get more information about where that location might be, we need to look everywhere. Since we can't do that by ourselves, the town is helping out. Live with it." The stern tone of his voice communicated that he didn't want to hear any more arguments.

His lips forming a tight line across his face, Joe appeared to be pouting. "Fine. But if somebody gets themselves killed wandering around on these back roads, it's not on my head." In a sudden move, he shot up from his seat. "Nadine isn't out there, is she?"

Eli shook his head. "Holly said that according to Sylvia, Nadine was adamant about going with them, but Sylvia talked her out of it. Apparently she told Nadine she had too much to lose if she went out and they crashed into a ditch or something. Don't worry, Sylvia put her foot down."

"Good," Joe sighed as he lowered himself back into his chair. "If something happened to her and the baby..." The anguish on his face told Eli he couldn't bring himself to finish the thought. "She was adamant about going, though?"

"Apparently," Eli said quietly. It wasn't often that he felt sympathetic for his surly friend, but in this case, he couldn't help himself. After Nadine's miscarriage earlier in the year, Joe had been beside himself. Never having pegged him as the father type, Eli had been surprised. Now that Nadine was pregnant again, and so far along this time, his friend worried so much that every time a gentle breeze blew, it would somehow cause another one.

"How could she be so careless?" he muttered to himself. "Doesn't she know it would have been dangerous for her to be out there?"

Taking a moment to decide if he should say anything, Eli finally decided he should. "Look man, put yourself in Nadine's shoes. A friend is missing. What would you do if you were in her shoes? My guess is you'd want to be out looking. Am I right?"

With sagging shoulders, Joe admitted that Eli was, in fact, correct.

Placing a comforting hand on Joe's shoulder, Eli quickly pulled it away to point at the computer screen. "Look at that!"

The two men stared intently at the image unfolding in front of them. As they watched, Marian pulled up on the street in front of Henry Feinstein's house. As she got out and began walking toward the front porch, they saw an old pickup truck pull into view. A heavily bearded man got out of the driver's side of the truck, caught up to Marian, and placed something that looked like a cloth over her nose and mouth. After several seconds, she went limp.

"Is he suffocating her?" Eli asked, adrenaline coursing through his veins. They wanted to find out what happened, but watching Marian get murdered on camera wasn't the way they wanted to see things play out.

Joe shook his head tightly, and never taking his eyes from the screen, said, "My guess is he drugged her with something."

The man turned away from the camera and effortlessly hoisted Marian onto his back. The ease with which he did it suggested a great amount of strength.

Watching in horror, they saw the man plunk Marian into the passenger side of the truck, circle around, slide in, and drive away.

"What now?" Eli asked.

Joe leaned back in his chair and laced his fingers behind his head. "First we list what we know. Marian was taken by a bearded man in an old truck." The two men locked eyes. "Are you thinking what I'm thinking?"

"This means Henry Feinstein is off the hook," Eli said.

"That, and we need to get Fred Rooney in here. Remember what he said about a bearded man buying the ingredients for Marian's buttered rum?"

Eli chewed on his lip. "And we basically told him he was crazy."

Silence filled the squad room before Joe broke it. "At least we know one thing. If the guy buying those ingredients is the same one we just saw on the video, Marian was still alive and well as of yesterday."

<h1 style="text-align:center">CHAPTER FIFTY-TWO</h1>

HER ARMS FULL of rusty, otherwise useless farm tools, Marian used her foot to shove open the back door to the farmhouse. Somewhere in the pile of things she'd scavenged from the barn, there had to be something she could turn into a nice gift for Vito.

It was too cold to stay out in the barn any longer, so anything that held potential was carried into the relative warmth of the farmhouse.

As Marian walked through the kitchen and living room to her own meager quarters, Vito raised an eyebrow in her direction. "What are you doing bringing that junk in here?" he queried, a look of intrigue on his face. "You're not planning to make some kind of weapon so you can escape, are you?"

With her best try at a look of indignation, Marian dropped her jaw and shook her head. "I would never!" With a smile and a wink, she turned away from the captor she'd grown so fond of and walked toward the musty old bedroom she'd been using the last few days. Lowering the armful of rusted metal to the floor, a muscle in the small of her back protested against the action. It had been much too cold to sort out everything thoroughly in the barn, and Marian began the task, fully aware that whatever she did would be time-consuming and tedious.

Finally, she picked up the rusty blade of a tiller. Inspiration struck, and she began humming "Santa Claus is Coming to Town." Marian ran her thumb over the rusty surface. It was porous from age, the blade dulled.

"Perfect," she muttered to herself through a satisfied smile.

All she would need was some paint and a clock kit to turn this useless piece of junk into a farmhouse-chic decorative item.

Setting it off to the side, she continued rummaging, surprised by how much she'd been able to carry. She was just about to lose hope of finding any more useful items, when she found a triangular dinner bell hooked on the handle of an old hoe. It looked to be made of cast iron, though years of neglect had left it tarnished. Tucking it under the hem of her borrowed flannel shirt, she rushed to the bathroom and closed the door. The lock was broken, so she'd have to be quick. Running warm water from the faucet, she began rinsing the bell. Though the water loosened some of the grime, it still needed more work. Marian grabbed an old scrub brush from under the sink and went to work removing the filth that clung to it. After several minutes of scrubbing, a still dull but cleaner triangle appeared. Squinting and bringing it closer to her face, she saw that the bell had been personalized.

Farmhouse Inn Bed & Breakfast.

"This old house used to be a bed-and-breakfast," Marian murmured, imagining the place providing a warm welcome to anyone who stayed here. She pictured a roaring fire in the nearly dilapidated fireplace and a tray of cookies or muffins on the counter in the kitchen, with coffee and tea nearby for anyone who was escaping the blustery winter winds. In the summer, she could imagine guests strolling around the expansive grounds, picking wildflowers or blackberries.

Marian's heart swelled with the thought. Guests must have had such good times here. That explained why there was an en suite bathroom for each bedroom and a large dining room. Her stomach clenched at its current sad state of disrepair. The good times she imagined were long gone.

What an interesting history this old place must have, she thought, vowing to herself that when she got out of here and things settled down, she'd find out more about that history.

Forcing the images of what the house used to be from her mind, she focused on the task at hand, making a mental list for the things she'd need to complete the tiller-blade clock. Considering that the place hadn't seen a paintbrush or roller in at least a decade, the chances of finding any usable paint was probably zero. Same with the clock kit.

Unless…

Marian shoved the tiller blade under the bed she'd been sleeping in and began meandering through the house. Maybe she could find an old clock that worked.

Pausing outside a bedroom that housed a sagging king-size bed, Marian took in the view of what was probably a garden at one time. A crooked birdbath sat among scrubby vines and a plethora of dead plants. She closed her eyes and imagined this room and the garden restored to their former beauty.

How very much like our culture, Marian thought. Old things are tossed out or abandoned instead of repaired. An image of Roger, giving his regular speech about what the world has come to, while shaking his head, floated through Marian's mind.

Roger would have loved to restore this place. Especially the garden. She could picture him sitting in this very room, early in the morning, gazing out the window at the flowers planted around the birdbath. Sadness washed over Marian, and she turned from the window and began checking closets and drawers for an old clock. In the last room, she finally found success. After a quick inspection, she realized that all the clock would need to work again was new batteries. Grabbing it in her small hands, Marian hustled back to her room and began disassembling the clock. The pieces scattered around her, she rebuilt it in her mind using the tiller blade and the pieces from the old clock.

It would look great when it was finished, but she'd need Vito to go to the hardware store.

Standing up and taking a moment to stretch the stiff muscles in her back, she went back out into the living room and found Vito lounging by the fire, a dusty old copy of an F. Scott Fitzgerald novel in his hands. He looked up as she approached.

"Not much to read around here," he complained as he closed the book and tossed it onto the ottoman that held his socked feet.

"I'm glad I'm not interrupting anything important, then," Marian said with a smile. "I need you to run to the hardware store."

A groan was Vito's first response. "In case you haven't noticed, we're covered with ice and snow. Besides that, I don't know that I should be showing my face all over town. What do you think you need?"

Marian shrugged and suppressed a chuckle at Vito's grouchiness. "Just batteries and some white chalk paint."

"You want me to go into town for that? It's hardly worth the trip."

"I haven't asked for much, and you have to admit I'm being a model prisoner," Marian urged with a lilt to her voice. "Please?"

With an exasperated exhale, Vito stood and went to put his shoes on. "That's it? Just batteries and white chalk paint?"

Nodding in the affirmative, Marian felt excited for the first time in days. Ideas swirling around in her head, she watched Vito open the door.

"Don't try anything," he warned as he walked out into the snow.

Even though she couldn't be at work, spreading Christmas cheer to the kids, she was still an elf. This time, the joy she was spreading was to a very lonely man who'd made some really bad choices.

CHAPTER FIFTY-THREE

DISCOURAGED FROM THEIR lack of progress, Sylvia and Holly slugged their way up Nadine and Joe's sidewalk. The text they'd gotten from Nadine a couple hours earlier told them to come over when they were finished searching for the day. She was making dinner for everyone, her contribution to the search efforts. Morale throughout the town was low, and Christmas was only thirty-six hours away. How would they ever bring Marian home in such a short amount of time when they had no idea where to look? For all they knew, she might not even be in Saddle Hill anymore.

Holly pressed the doorbell and the two looked at each other with weary eyes as they waited for Nadine or Joe to come to the door.

"I don't have much of an appetite," Holly said quietly.

"Neither do I," Sylvia responded, then added, "but Nadine was really upset that she couldn't help with the search. This is her way of helping us without risking her life or the baby's."

Holly nodded silently, then said, "I wonder what she made for dinner."

Shrugging, Sylvia murmured, "Whatever it is, I hope it's hot. I'm freezing."

"Me, too."

The sound of footsteps approaching from the other side of the door halted the conversation. Nadine, her face showing strain despite the welcoming smile plastered on her face, swung the door wide so Holly and Sylvia could enter.

"It smells delicious in here," Holly said, surprised that her appetite had returned.

"Thank you. I made chicken potpie, Marian's recipe. It always makes me think of her, and after being out in this weather half the day, I figured you'd want something to warm you from the inside out." This time Nadine's smile was genuine. The two women smiled back, instantly comforted by the care on Nadine's face.

"You always know the right thing to do," Sylvia said as they followed Nadine past the entryway and into the living room.

Holly's face lit up when she saw Eli stretched out on the sofa. "You're here! Do you have any leads on where Marian might be?"

The droop of Eli's mouth answered Holly's question.

"I see…" Holly replied, her frown mirroring Eli's.

He extended his arms toward her, and she sat down next to him, his arms enfolding her in a comforting hug.

"This is all so surreal," Holly said, shaking her head. "My life was miserable before I met Marian. I was making terrible choices and getting myself in so much trouble, then she took a chance on me and it changed my life. I finally knew what it was like to have someone truly care about me." A tear slipped down her cheek. "I can't lose her."

Eli pulled Holly closer and whispered, "Marian isn't the

only one that cares for you, Holly," as Sylvia, Nadine, and Joe retreated to the kitchen.

"Those two could use some privacy," Nadine said and busied herself setting the table.

"How did it go today?" Joe asked, his voice gruff.

Sylvia arched an eyebrow at him. "It was a bust."

"I could have told you it would be," he replied, his lips tight and voice dripping with annoyance.

Allowing her eyes to dart between Nadine and Joe, Sylvia asked hesitantly, "Is there a problem?"

Crossing his arms over his chest, Joe growled, "Only if you call civilians interfering with police business a problem."

Nadine gently smacked Joe's arm with the back of her hand. "What's gotten into you? The whole town loves Marian and is volunteering their time to help find her. Volunteers help search for missing folks all the time. Why is it a problem now?"

He dropped his hands to his sides and his shoulders hunched forward, a move that those closest to him recognized as defeat. "Because the roads are treacherous, and the last thing we need is for people to get themselves killed trying to be a hero."

"A hero?" Sylvia spat. "You think people are out looking for Marian because they want to be a *hero*? Is that what you're trying to be? Wake up, Joe. People are risking their lives because they care about her. This isn't about us—any of us. How could you even think that?"

Pointing a finger into Sylvia's face, his face a deep crimson, Joe growled, "How dare you think the reason I'm doing this is for any other reason than getting her home?"

Nadine stepped between them. "Stop it! Both of you," she commanded. "I know we're all stressed and scared right now but yelling at each other won't solve anything."

"You're right. I'm sorry," Sylvia said, extending a hand as a peace offering toward Joe. "Truce?"

He accepted her outstretched hand and mumbled, "Truce."

"Good," Nadine said, stepping out from between her husband and friend. "Dinner is ready." She pulled a steaming dish of potpie out of the oven and placed it on a trivet in the middle of the dining room table. "Holly and Eli, come eat," Nadine called.

Everyone took their places at the table and said a brief prayer for Marian's safe return. As Nadine dished out the potpie, Sylvia asked cautiously, "So, has there been any information about Marian?"

Joe sat the plate Nadine had just given him on his place mat and turned his eyes, still oozing disapproval, toward Sylvia. "We have some new information, but I don't know what to do with it."

Holly looked from Joe to Eli. "Spill it. Maybe we can help you think through things."

Eli glanced toward his partner and gave an encouraging nod. "It can't hurt."

With a sigh, Joe leaned back in his chair and crossed his arms again. "We thought Henry Feinstein might have had something to do with it since he was so hateful to Marian before she disappeared. Paranoid man that he is, he's got security cameras set up around his house. He came in with his lawyer and gave us permission to access the footage. Turns out, Henry was telling the truth when he said he didn't have anything to do with whatever happened to Marian. The images show an old truck and a man with a bushy beard holding something over Marian's face and carrying her off to his truck."

"Why didn't you say anything sooner?" Holly shrieked. "Who was the guy? Did you recognize him?"

Eli placed a restraining hand on Holly's arm. "Settle down. We don't know who he is, though he does match the description of a man Fred Rooney said came into the market and bought ingredients for Marian's apparently top-secret hot buttered rum."

"Do you have a picture of the man and the truck?" Sylvia asked. "That way we can keep an eye out for him while we're searching tomorrow."

Joe pulled his cell from his back pocket and began swiping through pictures. "There," he said, plopping the phone in the middle of the table right next to the dish of potpie.

The three women stood slightly from their chairs and leaned over the table. After studying the picture for a moment, Nadine gasped. Sylvia and Holly followed suit.

"What is it?" Eli asked, glancing between them.

"We saw this truck yesterday!" Nadine yelled.

Sitting bolt upright in his chair, Joe demanded, "Where? Why were you anywhere near this truck?"

"When we were out looking for Marian yesterday, we stopped at this dumpy old farmhouse way on the outskirts of town. A man with a big beard answered the door when we knocked." Nadine frowned. "He told us he hadn't seen her."

"Of course he'd say that," Joe bellowed. "He couldn't exactly say, 'Come on in. Meet the woman I drugged and kidnapped. I'm sure she'd love the company.' Where is this house?" he asked urgently.

"I don't know the address and it's hard to explain. I'll have to come with you," Sylvia offered.

"I'm coming, too," Holly said.

Eli shook his head firmly. "You stay here with Nadine. See

if you can remember anything else. Call my cell if you come up with anything."

Holly nodded in agreement and whispered, "Please be careful."

"Of course," Eli said, dropping a kiss on Holly's forehead. "Maybe you two could whip up some hot chocolate for us to have when we get back." He winked and then the trio was gone, leaving the chicken potpie untouched.

Nadine and Holly put their arms around one another, and Holly whispered, "Please let this be the Christmas miracle we've been hoping for."

As the second hand of the clock ticked by in the otherwise silent house, it felt like they, along with the rest of the town, were holding their breath waiting for their miracle to happen.

CHAPTER FIFTY-FOUR

"DO YOU THINK she'll like it?" Kris asked his parents as they all sat together around the roaring fire in the living room.

"It's lovely," Patricia said, admiring the scarf Kris had purchased earlier in the day for Carol.

"I've never had a girlfriend at Christmas before. Any special occasion, actually, so I don't exactly know what to get. This scarf just reminded me of her. The colors are so rich and it's beautiful, in an exotic kind of way.

Patricia smiled at her son. "Then tell her that. I'm sure the reason you chose this particular gift will mean just as much to her as the gift itself."

James snorted from behind the newspaper he was reading in his favorite chair next to the fireplace.

"What was that for?" Patricia admonished.

Lowering the newspaper, James took off his reading glasses and stroked his thick white beard. "If you want my opinion, which I know nobody does, I wouldn't waste my time or money on that woman."

"James! Don't say things like that. Can't you see how happy she makes our son?"

"Yeah, Dad," Kris interjected. "What did she ever do to you? You don't even know her."

James raised the newspaper and muttered, "I know enough."

Red creeping toward his receding hairline, Kris stood up and jerked the newspaper away from his father. "I'm not good enough for her, is that it? News flash, I already know that. She's beautiful and successful, and I'm a part-time Santa with thinning hair. But I'll be done with school soon, and then I'll be able to get a real job that I can be proud of."

James's face turned the same color red as his son's. "Hold on. Since when is being Santa not a respectable job? Don't start on this again, Kris. Also, it has nothing to do with whether or not you're good enough for her. The problem is, she's not good enough for you. You have a good heart, even though you're grumpy half the time, and you care about people. I get the feeling she only cares about herself."

"You have a lot of nerve," Kris shouted, his hands balled into fists. He whirled around to face Patricia. "Mom, tell him he's wrong about Carol."

"Well, Kris," Patricia said with a shrug. "Your father has a point. From the few times I've seen her, she seems like a taker who gives very little, if any, of herself."

"How dare you!" Kris bellowed as he stomped toward the front door, snatched up his coat and rammed his feet into his boots. "You're wrong about her, both of you!"

As he opened the door, Patricia said softly, "Think about it, Kris. What have you given her? What has she given you in return? We love you, son, and we want you to be careful. Love isn't something you have a lot of experience with."

"And if you had your way I never would!" With that, Kris jerked open the door and disappeared into the cold winter night.

James and Patricia exchanged glances. "And here we thought that once the kids were grown it would be easier to be their parents," James said wryly.

"I guess he hasn't seen the story in the paper. My bet is she got the information for it from him," Patricia said solemnly.

James nodded in agreement and kept his gaze on the door. "He has no idea how much we hope we're wrong about her."

The knot that sat in each of their stomachs told them they weren't.

Kris clutched the steering wheel until the skin on his knuckles hurt. How could his parents say such terrible things about the woman he'd fallen for? Yes, it was true that he and Carol couldn't possibly be more different. That didn't mean they were wrong for each other, though. In fact, some of the best love stories in history were between polar opposites.

Just look at Shakespeare's plays, he thought. You can't get more different than *Romeo and Juliet*. That worked out. I mean, sure, they both killed themselves, but that wasn't real life.

The back of his car skidded on a patch of ice, and he nearly careened into a ditch on his right. His heart thumping in his chest, he squeezed the steering wheel even tighter as he regained control. Now that he had someone in his life that made him excited for each moment, he couldn't afford to die.

His phone dinged from the cup holder, indicating someone had sent him a text message. Refusing to tear his eyes away from the icy road, he ignored it. It was probably his mom or dad trying to apologize for saying mean things about Carol, anyway. He was still too angry to talk to them.

After what seemed like forever, he finally pulled into the parking lot of his apartment complex. He'd just go inside, put on his flannel pants, make some hot chocolate, and call Carol. As crazy as it sounded, after feeling like he had to defend her to his parents, he wanted to hear her prove to him that she did care about him and wasn't just using him.

Clad in flannel with a steaming cup of cocoa in his hand, he finally checked his phone to see what kind of lame apology his parents tried to make. To his delight, he saw that it was Carol who had sent the text. His heart sank, however, when he read the words.

Turning in early. Talk to you in the morning.

"That was chilly," Kris mumbled as he reread the words. He wasn't the mushy sort, but that was impersonal, even for his taste. Dread worked its way into his chest. *Were Mom and Dad right about her?*

Shaking his head vigorously, he reminded himself that the feeling behind text messages was often misunderstood. He allowed his eyes to wander off the words and settle on the kissy-face emoji at the end of the message. A smile lifted the corners of his mouth. That was proof that she cared. People don't send the kissy face to just anybody, he reasoned.

Sighing contentedly, he took a sip of the hot chocolate and leaned back in his chair. Propping his feet up on the ottoman, he pictured Carol's face when he gave her the scarf. She would look beautiful in it.

But was it enough?

Closing his eyes, he began humming a Christmas song. Surprised by it, he realized that with Carol by his side this Christmas, he finally understood the real reason people love the season so much.

CHAPTER FIFTY-FIVE

NADINE AND HOLLY sat shoulder to shoulder on the sofa, staring absently at the TV as it played a random Christmas movie that took place in an idyllic small town much like Saddle Hill. While the snow fell on the scene unfolding on the television, the two friends couldn't stop hoping that Marian would be home tonight.

"Will they find her?" Nadine asked.

Holly reached over and grabbed Nadine's hand. "They have to. I need her."

Nadine gave her hand a squeeze. "We all need her. Joe and Eli will bring her home. Don't worry."

Holly took a deep breath and nodded, then turned her attention back to the movie. Just as the main character was about to announce his undying love for the single mom with a heartbreaking past, Nadine's phone rang. She picked it up off the coffee table and glanced at the screen.

"It's Joe," she said just before she tapped the screen to answer the call. "Hey, did you get her?"

Holly watched as Nadine's eyebrows furrowed. The worry

lines on her forehead deepened as she listened to what Joe was saying.

Unable to wait any longer, Holly tapped Nadine's arm and motioned for her to clue her in on what was happening. When Nadine didn't respond, Holly shook her arm and mouthed, "Put it on speaker."

With narrowed eyes and a firm shake of her head, Nadine turned her back on her friend. "I'll tell her. Be careful. I love you," Nadine said, then disconnected the call.

"What is it? Did they get her?" Holly pressed, unable to keep the hope from her voice.

Nadine turned back toward Holly, her eyes filled with tears.

Holly felt her stomach drop. "What? What happened? Did they not find Marian? Did they find her but she wasn't okay?" The questions were rapid-fire, but she couldn't stop her anxiety from spilling out of her mouth. She put one hand on her stomach and covered her mouth with the other. She felt sick.

Shaking her head slowly, Nadine whispered, "They didn't make it there."

The room seemed to spin. Holly gulped, then, needing an outlet for her ever-increasing fear, stood and began pacing around the living room. "What do you mean they didn't make it there? What happened? Are they okay? Is Eli okay?"

"They're fine. Apparently the roads out there are impassable. They won't be able to get to Marian until they can have somebody clear them."

Holly stopped pacing and put her hands on her hips. "Surely they can't be that bad. Just tell them to go slower," Holly argued.

Hoisting herself off the sofa and taking a moment to rub her lower back, Nadine took a few steps toward her friend and stopped. "They can't." Nadine's eyes dropped to the slippers that encased her swollen feet. "They were in an accident."

Putting one uncertain foot in front of the other, Holly managed to stagger to the sofa and drop into it. Her eyes were wide and her face pale, making her freckles look several shades darker than they usually did. "How bad? Are they okay?"

Nadine bit her lip and lowered herself next to Holly. "For the most part they're fine. They slid off the road and hit a utility pole." She reached across and grasped Holly's hand. "Eli got the worst of it, I'm afraid. They're waiting for an ambulance."

Holly's mouth suddenly felt like cotton, and her stomach roiled. Her legs trembled so violently that they wouldn't support her even if she needed them to. "Is he okay? I should meet him at the hospital." Willing her legs to hold her, she stood and tripped over her own feet as she raced toward the door.

Moving as quickly as her bulging stomach would allow, Nadine intercepted her and helped her back to the sofa. "They aren't even there yet. Joe thinks his car is totaled, so they'll probably have to hitch a ride with the paramedics. We'll both go to meet them at the hospital. The first thing we have to do, though, is get our heads on straight. It won't help anybody if we rush out of here and get into an accident ourselves. Take a few minutes to breathe and focus on what you can do to be the most help."

Holly shot Nadine a look that said waiting was the last thing she wanted to do, but did as her friend suggested. After taking several deep breaths, her mind was clearer and her body felt calmer. "How did you get to be so wise?" she asked as she stood on legs that were finally stable enough to hold her.

Nadine shrugged. "Just by living life, I guess. I've learned a lot this past year." She grabbed her keys and the two went to Nadine's car.

Instead of welcoming Marian home tonight, they'd be welcoming Joe, Eli, and Sylvia to the hospital. Trying to focus on being there for them, Nadine refused to think about Marian not coming home tonight, or that their Christmas miracle would have to wait.

CHAPTER FIFTY-SIX

SYLVIA GROANED AND rubbed the back of her neck while she turned her head from side to side. After being given a once-over by the paramedics, she and Joe were deemed good to go home with no further treatment necessary.

Eli was a different story.

They suspected he'd suffered a concussion when the car skidded on the ice and slammed into a telephone pole. Eli, who was sitting in the front passenger side, took the brunt of the impact. Sylvia had been sitting behind Joe, and though she'd been jerked around, her seatbelt had caught. Fortunately, they didn't think she had anything worse than a few bruises and possibly a minor case of whiplash.

Joe had a small abrasion on his forehead from the airbag deploying but seemed fine. They were all shaken up, but thankfully there didn't seem to be any life-threatening injuries.

In the waiting room, Sylvia and Joe sat together while Eli was given a more thorough exam, making sure they didn't miss any internal trauma.

The doors of the emergency room whooshed open and

Holly and Nadine rushed in. Holly's eyes searched the room wildly and met Sylvia's. Clutching her shoulder bag tightly against her body with her elbow, Holly hurried toward her.

"Where's Eli?" Holly demanded, her voice quivering with emotion.

Sylvia stood slowly, her stiff back protesting the action. "The doctor is still checking him out. Come sit here with me," she said, lowering herself gingerly back into the hard wooden chair. "Whoever designed this room certainly didn't anticipate people having a long wait time, did they? Either that or they were a bunch of sadists."

Sylvia realized her attempt at a joke fell flat as Holly's eyes were still scanning the room, as if she anticipated that Eli would pop up out of nowhere.

"Working yourself up won't help Eli. When they let him go, he's going to need to see your smiling face, not you being freaked out because he's got a few bumps and bruises. Can you handle that?" Sylvia asked gently. She reached out and grabbed Holly's hand, giving her a tug toward the chair. This time Holly agreed.

As she settled into the chair and hugged her bag to her chest, Holly allowed her eyes to wander around the room where it settled on a sad little Christmas tree with a few colored lights strung around it. "It certainly isn't very cheery in here."

Sylvia shrugged. "No, it isn't. I guess people that find themselves in the emergency room aren't feeling too cheery, though."

Holly shook her head absently. "I guess not." She swiped at her eyes with the back of her hand. "This is turning out to be the worst Christmas ever, and I've known some bad Christmases," she muttered.

Sylvia gave her hand another squeeze. "It will be okay, Holly. Please don't give up hope. We know where Marian has been all this time and that she was fine a day or so ago. We'll get her back. And Eli will be fine. You're not going to be able to get rid of him that easily." Sylvia winked at her friend. "In fact, I don't think you'll ever be able to get rid of him."

Rubbing her hands on her thighs, Holly exhaled and leaned back in her chair. "Why are terrible things happening to people I love? Christmas has always been like this for me. My parents split at Christmas, and I've spent so many alone that I sort of got used to it, you know? Now Marian, who is more like a mother to me than my own mother ever was, is missing. And Eli…"

Sylvia draped her arm around Holly's shoulders and pulled her close. "You love him, don't you?"

A dry chuckle escaped Holly's throat. "Yeah, I do. A lot. Maybe I shouldn't. I've always thought he was way too good for me and that one of these days he'd wake up and realize what kind of girl I am—or was—but I can't help myself. He seems to look past all that. No guy has ever been able to look beyond what I've done. Apparently I find that irresistible."

"Don't sell yourself short, sweetie. Eli is over the moon for you. As far as he's concerned, you're the only one for him."

Holly could feel the rush of color sweep up her neck and onto her cheeks. "Yeah?"

"Yeah. Now stop worrying. He's a tough guy, and it seems as though he's got a lot to live for."

"Thanks," Holly said, giving Sylvia a quick hug. As Holly released her, she looked up into the serious face of a doctor who was approaching her from the direction of the exam rooms.

Joe rose on unsteady legs and pulled Nadine into a tight hug.

"I'm so glad you're okay," Nadine whispered into his neck. "I don't know what we would have done without you." A tear squeezed out her eye and rolled down her cheek, then soaked into Joe's jacket.

His hands sliding from her back to her stomach, he choked out, "For a second, when we were sliding and I couldn't control the car, I thought about you and this little one, and the possibility of not being there to watch him grow up. It scared me, Nay. What if things had gone differently and I didn't make it back tonight? What would you do? What would the baby do?"

Nadine cupped her hands on Joe's face and forced him to look in her eyes. "Everything is fine. You're safe, Sylvia is safe, and Eli is safe. Just because you're banged up a little doesn't mean you were in danger of leaving us."

"But things could have very easily gone differently tonight," he challenged.

"True," Nadine agreed, "but you could just as easily slip on a step and crack your head. None of us are guaranteed tomorrow. But I still have you and you still have us." She rubbed a circle on her belly for emphasis.

"So, how close did you get to the farmhouse where we think Marian is being held?"

Joe let out an exasperated sigh. "Not close enough. The roads out that way are terrible. Nobody could get out there until the plows and salt trucks clear the way. Knowing where she might be and being helpless to get to her is a terrible feeling. I can only hope whoever has her is treating her okay."

Nadine laid a hand on Joe's arm. "You'll get her tomorrow.

I know you will. If there's one thing I know about you, it's that nothing can stop you once you've set your mind on something." She smiled at her husband with adoration evident in her face.

Warmth spread through Joe's body. Nobody else had ever looked at him that way. Nadine, the sweetest and most beautiful woman he'd ever met, thought he could do anything. It shocked him that he could feel so proud and so inadequate at the same time.

The couple looked toward Holly and Sylvia, who were locked in a hug. Their gaze traveled past the two friends as a doctor approached.

"He looks serious," Nadine whispered nervously.

"He's an ER doc. They always look serious. I guess they'd have to, after all the terrible things they see," Joe assured her.

"I guess so," Nadine said with a shrug. "Let's go see what he has to say about Eli."

⌁

An hour later, Joe and Nadine, Holly, Eli, and Sylvia were crammed into Nadine's car on the way back home. Eli had a concussion and several cuts and bruises, but the doctor assured them all that he'd be fine, though he could expect to be sore for the next week or so.

Holly sat between Eli and Sylvia in the backseat, her fingers intertwined with Eli's. They'd agreed that he'd stay at Joe and Nadine's house, and since the doctor recommended that he didn't sleep because of the concussion, Holly volunteered to be there to keep him awake.

Sylvia's dark eyes were heavy, exhaustion evident in her pretty face. The last several days had taken a toll on all of them, and it seemed like the accident was the cherry on top of all the things that had happened. Citing exhaustion, the group decided that Sylvia would stay in the Adlers' guest room. Though the small house would be crowded, everyone felt better not having to be alone.

Nadine pulled the car into the garage, and with groans and stiff bodies, the group got out of the car and trudged inside the house. Within minutes, everyone but Holly and Eli were tucked into warm beds, putting aside the excitement of the day. Holly, taking seriously her task of keeping Eli awake, brought several games out of the coat closet.

As she shuffled a deck of cards, she stole a glance at the man who'd done the impossible and gotten past her barriers. She had a family here in Saddle Hill. Marian had been the first person to take a chance on her, and she had to make sure Eli was well enough to bring her home.

CHAPTER FIFTY-SEVEN

KRIS JINGLE ADJUSTED the plates on the table and placed a neatly wrapped box next to one of them. He was having breakfast with Carol before all the other family festivities began later today, and he wanted it to be perfect. It would be just the two of them this morning, and his stomach flip-flopped when he thought about giving the gift he'd carefully chosen to her.

Though he felt like he knew her fairly well, she was a woman that was full of surprises and certainly kept him guessing most of the time.

It was one of the things he liked most about her.

Glancing at the clock on the microwave, he noted that it was almost nine o'clock. Carol should be there in just a few minutes. He pulled the pan of biscuits from the oven and piled them into a breadbasket, then retrieved the bowl of cut fruit from the refrigerator. Next, he opened the package of bacon and laid the strips out on his electric griddle, which had been a gift from his mother last Christmas. As they sizzled,

"

he dumped the eggs he'd already whipped into the skillet and topped them with cheese, ham, and green onions. Breakfast was the only thing he could make that was consistently appetizing, and omelets were his specialty.

He flipped the omelets onto a plate, scooted the bacon from the griddle to the same plate as the omelets, and placed them on the table. Setting the plate on the table, he surveyed the setup one last time.

"Looks good," he muttered, glad he'd taken the time to buy a small, potted poinsettia for the middle of the table. He wanted this to be a Christmas to remember, and with Carol by his side, he was certain it would be.

Taking a deep breath and smiling at his good fortune, his moment of contentment was interrupted by a knock at the door. Before he reached it, the knob turned and Carol walked in. With a smile on her face, she nudged the door closed behind her.

"It smells great in here," she gushed as she stepped into Kris's outstretched arms. "You never told me you were a cook."

Kris felt his face flush, and he shrugged one shoulder. "I've got to keep you on your toes," he said, burying his nose into her hair. Releasing her from the embrace, he intertwined his fingers with hers and led her to the kitchen, where the food tempted their hungry bellies. Kris pulled a chair out for Carol and scooted it back under the table once she'd settled in.

His efforts were rewarded with a megawatt smile. "Such a gentleman," she said with a wink and dropped her napkin into her lap.

Kris sat in his own chair and followed her lead with his napkin. As Carol helped herself to a biscuit and bacon, Kris cut a wedge of the omelet and slid it onto her plate. "This is my favorite omelet. I hope you like it as much as I do."

"I'm sure I will," Carol assured him as she broke the biscuit in half and slathered butter and jam on both sides. "I don't get home-cooked meals very often when I'm out on assignment, so this is a real treat. Even the breakfasts at the nicer hotels I stay at seem to be missing something." She picked up her fork and speared a piece of omelet, then popped it into her mouth. "Oh, that's good," she commented, her eyes wide.

Kris felt his face flush again. He had to get control of that or she would think he was some kind of simpering doormat of a man who lived for others to tell him he was good enough. He already knew she was out of his league. The last thing he needed to do was communicate that to her and give her second thoughts.

He filled his plate with food and began eating. Carol was right. The meal was delicious. He picked up a piece of bacon, crisped to perfection, just the way he liked it, and took a bite. Not the healthiest breakfast, but it was a special occasion. Keeping an eye on the middle-aged paunch that was threatening to take up residence in his midsection would have to wait until after the holidays.

When their plates were empty, Kris refilled their coffee cups and reached for Carol's hand. "Our time together this past month has been the happiest time of my life," Kris said, not even caring that the naked adoration spilling from his face could make him look like he was desperately in love with this woman.

He was.

Carol answered by squeezing his fingers and leaning forward to brush a soft kiss on his jawline.

Using his other hand, Kris nudged the small, wrapped package toward Carol. "Finding a gift for someone as amazing as you is no easy feat. But I think I finally did."

"You didn't have to get me anything," Carol protested as she picked up the box and turned it over in her hands.

"I wanted to. I want you to know how much you mean to me. My life is better because you're in it," Kris said tenderly.

This time it was Carol whose face flushed. She tore the paper off the box and opened it, revealing a bracelet with multiple charms dangling from it, nestled on the scarf Kris had so lovingly chosen for her. She removed it from the box and studied it carefully, smiling as she realized what each of the charms represented. He'd chosen charms that chronicled their time together, from that first meeting in the parking lot when he backed into her car to now, their first Christmas together. "It's beautiful," she said, her eyes brimmed with tears. "You really shouldn't have. This is too much."

"I disagree," Kris countered softly. "It's not enough."

Carol stood and pushed her chair back, walking to the living room to retrieve her shoulder bag. She withdrew a rectangular box, wrapped in red and gold with a big gold bow on it. Settling back into her chair, she gave the package to Kris, and looked on as he opened it. In his hands he held a leather-bound book, embossed with gold letters on the front. *The Complete Works of William Shakespeare.*

"Carol, this is beautiful."

"I know you already have everything he's written, but I had this one specially bound for you. I hope you like it."

Kris's gaze wandered to the bottom right corner. There, in gold letters much smaller than the title, was his name. She'd had this personalized for him.

He stood and threw his arms around her, picked her up and swung her around. "This is the best gift I've ever received. Thank you."

"You're very welcome." Glancing at her wrist, Carol gasped. "Oh, no. I have to go. I'm covering the town's festivities today, and I have a few errands to run before I get started."

Kris's smile fell and he felt as though someone had just knocked the wind out of him. "Do you have to leave?"

The corner of Carol's mouth drooped. "I'm afraid so. I'll see you later, though." With that, she gathered her things, planted a quick kiss on Kris's mouth, then dashed off, just as she'd done before.

Standing there in his living room, perplexed at why she always seemed to be leaving in such a hurry, he allowed the feeling of warmth that came with being near her to wash away the gnawing sense that something was wrong. With a sigh, he turned toward the kitchen and began putting the leftovers away. His gaze settling on the book Carol had just given him, he pushed his doubts away. She knew what he'd like and had given him the perfect gift.

Everything would be just fine, he knew it.

CHAPTER FIFTY-EIGHT

MARIAN WOKE UP to the sunshine gleaming through the window Christmas Eve morning. After a late night of putting the finishing touches on the gift she wanted to give to Vito, she'd finally drifted off to sleep on the lumpy and musty-smelling mattress, her final prayer for the night being that God would find a way to have her home before Christmas.

Fighting the sinking feeling that it was a prayer that wouldn't be answered, Marian decided to put on her cheeriest smile.

Grow where you're planted.

Marian smiled. "Merry Christmas, Roger," she whispered. It had been unexpected, but she had certainly been comforted by the words of wisdom he'd given her many times over the decades. She never would have guessed that it would be her deceased husband whose words would be bringing her the most comfort while she was being held against her will in a broken-down farmhouse that smelled like years of neglect.

Determined to make it a good day no matter where she spent it, Marian got out of bed and changed her clothes.

Carefully wrapping the clock she'd made out of the tiller blade in a blanket, Marian made her way out to the living room. There would be no tree to put the gift under, but she'd make do.

In the main living area, Marian was surprised to see a fire blazing in the fireplace and a small evergreen tree standing in the corner. There were no ornaments, but lights twinkled on the boughs.

Vito, his feet propped up on an ottoman, sat gazing into the fire, a thoughtful look on his face.

"Merry Christmas Eve," Marian chirped in her best effort to be the elf she'd been for so long.

A small smile tugged at the corners of Vito's mouth but didn't quite reach his eyes. "Merry Christmas Eve to you, too." His eyes settled on what appeared to be a folded blanket in her arms. "It's plenty warm out here. You didn't need to bring a blanket."

Marian took several steps forward and settled into a chair next to Vito. "This is for you."

"A blanket? You're giving me a smelly old blanket?" Amusement danced in his eyes.

"Of course not," Marian countered. "I didn't have any wrapping paper, so I had to improvise." She extended the makeshift package to Vito, who hesitantly accepted it.

"I know this isn't how you'd prefer to spend your Christmas Eve," Vito said, his words laced with sadness. "Honestly, it's not how I'd prefer to spend it, either. I hope you know by now that holding someone captive isn't my idea of a good time."

"I know that," Marian assured him.

I did the best I could at making the place feel festive this morning. While I was at the hardware store, I picked up the last strand of lights they had and wrapped them around this sad little tree I found in the woods."

"You don't know how much I appreciate that. Now, please open your gift," she urged.

Vito reluctantly began unfolding the blanket.

"Be careful, it's sharp," Marian warned.

Lifting an eyebrow at her, Vito continued his task. He flipped back the last flap of blanket and breathed, "Whoa, that's cool. You made this?"

Feeling herself beaming from the inside out, Marian knew she'd done the right thing.

Vito lifted the tiller-blade clock from the blanket and inspected the gift. It was rusty from sitting in the drafty old barn for who knows how long, but a coat of white chalk paint covered it nicely while still leaving the rustic look.

"I hope you like it. I couldn't exactly go Christmas shopping, so I had to work with what I had."

Vito dropped his head. "It's perfect, and completely undeserved."

Marian scooted closer to him and put a comforting hand on his arm. "I know this isn't who you are. You're not a kidnapper. You're not a criminal of any kind. I think you're just a nice guy who was in a desperate situation and got in over his head."

"I didn't give you anything for Christmas other than sadness. Some nice guy I am," he muttered.

Giving his arm a squeeze, Marian reminded him that things could have been much worse. "You could have meant harm for me, and you didn't. Despite being unable to leave the property, you've given me freedom to move around the house and let me poke around in the barn. This is not nearly as bad as it could have been."

Vito raised his eyes to meet Marian's. "I've sure made a mess of things, but I don't know how to make things right."

"The only thing we can ever do is the next right thing," Marian reminded him.

Vito nodded slowly and muttered to himself, "The next right thing." He swung his feet off the ottoman and stood from his position in the chair. "I can do that. I should have done it days ago."

Her brows furrowed in confusion, Marian asked, "What's that?"

His hands on his hips, he looked around the house. "I can let you go. I can give you what you really want, which is to be home for Christmas."

Marian jumped to her feet. "You would do that for me?"

Vito's eyes locked onto hers. "I'm not a monster. I don't want anything bad to happen to you." With brisk steps, he walked toward the front door and unlocked it with the key that had been dangling on a chain around his neck. "Go," he said, jerking his head toward the waiting world. "I'll call the sheriff and tell him where to find you so you won't get lost and freeze to death."

Marian threw her arms around Vito's neck. "I knew you were a good man."

As she turned to walk through the front door, a gasp and a thump behind her made her whirl around. There, in a crumpled ball, lay her captor, blood oozing from a gash on his forehead.

"Vito!" Marian shouted, then stooped over him, checking his neck for a pulse. Though faint, it was there. She breathed a sigh of relief as she looked around wildly in search of some clue about what had happened to him.

She stood and strong hands twisted her arms behind her back as the intruder deftly wound duct tape around her wrists. Before she could utter a protest, Marian was gagged and dragged past Vito's crumpled form and thrust into a chair. With the skill of a ranch hand tying up a calf, ropes were looped around Marian's body from shoulders to ankles until she was completely immobile.

"The fool should have known better than to try to let you go," the raspy voice said.

Marian twisted until she could see the assailant. A black ski mask covered the entire face. Even if this was someone she was familiar with, the disguise made it impossible to know who it was.

Marian tried to speak, but realized it was a lost cause when the only sounds that made it around the gag were grunts and moans.

It was useless.

"At least before, you had freedom to move around and that stupid oaf to take care of you. Now you're on your own. Given the fact that you no longer have access to food, water, or heat, I'm guessing it won't take more than a couple days for you to die. Too bad. From all I've heard about you, you'll be missed." At that, the masked intruder turned and walked out the front door, slamming it shut. It seemed a final punctuation to the threat.

The lock clicked and Marian knew she was in trouble. Fighting the fear that she would die before she was ever found, she closed her eyes and tried to take deep, steadying breaths through her nose.

It would all be over soon. One way or another.

CHAPTER FIFTY-NINE

SNOW FLURRIES GLITTERED in the morning sun as the unofficial Saddle Hill search party gathered at the entrance to the mall. Unwilling to be kept out of the loop, Joe and Eli stood in the center of the crowd, doing their best to contain the excitement of the group. The sense of urgency was palpable as everyone discussed the fact that it was Christmas Eve. No one mentioned their own plans for the day, since doing so brought a pang of guilt to everyone for having the luxury of celebrating the holiday in their own homes with their families.

For some reason he couldn't name, Eli had a hunch that the time for finding Marian alive and well was running out. It had been three days since Marian had gone missing, and he was keenly aware that the first twenty-four hours after a kidnapping was crucial.

"What if we don't find her?" a concerned townsperson said.

"I can't even bear to think about it," said another.

"Holly will be devastated if we don't get her back. The whole town will," someone chimed in.

Eli's gut clenched. Holly would be devastated if they

weren't able to get to Marian today. He would do anything he had to in order to keep her from experiencing that kind of pain.

His focus shifted as Sylvia and Ralph joined the group. Sylvia, stunning as always, wore a worried frown on her beautiful face. Her hair was pulled off to the side in a braid, a red wool toboggan hat covering her dark brown waves. Despite the age difference, Holly had become very fond of Sylvia the past year. Nadine, too. Everyone in town seemed thrilled to have her there, for that matter. She certainly brought a bit of class to the town, not to mention helping to boost the economy by partnering with Ralph on a line of jewelry for her fashion business.

He tore his gaze away from Sylvia and allowed it to settle on Ralph. With his round midsection and receding hairline, he certainly wasn't much to look at. Regardless of his physical shortcomings, though, the man had a heart of gold and never missed an opportunity to help a friend or neighbor.

From behind, a hand grabbed his elbow and he turned to see Holly, her adorable face set with worry. Though she was twenty-six to his twenty-four, she could have easily passed for nineteen. The splattering of freckles across the bridge of her nose only added to her youthful appearance.

"We need to get out there and find Marian," Holly urged. "I've had a bad feeling since I woke up this morning. Marian needs us to get to her soon."

Taking in her wide green eyes and pupils the size of dinner plates, he could tell she had the same nagging fear he did.

Marian was in trouble.

Carla stepped forward, and in a loud voice said, "Thank you all for coming out again today. As you all know, this is

Christmas Eve, and Marian would love nothing more than to be able to celebrate Christmas in her own house. The best way to make sure that happens is to break off into groups of two or three, searching places we didn't look yesterday." She paused and motioned toward Joe and Eli. "I want to thank Sheriff Adler and Deputy Nolan for being here with us to help direct the search. Before we get going, I know Sheriff Adler has a few words to say." Carla stepped into the background to allow all eyes to be turned toward Joe.

"Thanks, Carla. We have it on good authority that Marian is being held at an old house near Broken Branch Road. The roads out that way are treacherous, and I cannot warn you strongly enough to stay away from there. Deputy Nolan and I had a little mishap last night trying to get out there." Joe looked around and saw concerned faces staring back at him. "We have every confidence that we'll have Marian back home in time for dinner tonight. When that happens, we want to organize a 'Welcome Home' she'll never forget." He looked around and noticed the smiles his comment brought. "Now, let's go find her and bring her home. Stay safe, everybody." Joe issued the reminder even though he knew the other members of the search party wouldn't be on the most dangerous stretch of road in town.

People dispersed, Ralph and Carla leaving together. Eli turned toward Holly. "Coming?"

She shook her head tightly. "I have to stay here and man the store for Ralph. I wish I didn't. Finding Marian is the only thing I can think about."

Eli draped an arm around Holly's shoulder and pulled her close. "We'll find her. We're going back out to the property where you saw that old truck and the man with the beard.

As long as he hasn't moved her, there's a good chance we'll be bringing her home today."

"Thank you for that," Holly said quietly. "I've been a nervous wreck ever since she went missing. I don't know what I'd do without her."

Eli watched as Holly's eyes welled with tears. "Today's not the day you'll have to find out," he promised. Dropping a kiss on the top of her head, he said a quick goodbye and went with Joe and Sylvia to his pickup truck.

Chains were on the tires, and they were ready for the bad roads. With a backward glance toward Holly, Eli made a silent vow to stop at nothing to put a smile back on her face.

The morning sun had done its job of thawing some of the ice on Broken Branch Road. Though it was still slippery and required extra caution, the daylight made the road passable. Sylvia unsuccessfully tried to squelch the hope rising in her chest. If the information was right and nothing had changed, Marian would be sleeping in her own bed tonight.

Despite the truck having four-wheel drive and chains on the tires, they skidded and fishtailed multiple times on the way to the farmhouse. As they got closer, Sylvia couldn't shake the feeling that they were on the right track. That certainty was followed by mental scolding for being this close to Marian two days ago and not actually finding her.

As they pulled off the twisty main road onto an ice-and-gravel-covered driveway, Eli thrust a finger near her face from the backseat. "That's it!" he shouted. "That's the truck we saw on Henry Feinstein's camera footage."

Sylvia's stomach did a flip and her knees began to tremble.

What would the bearded man's reaction be when they showed up to rescue Marian? Joe and Eli were armed, but she was just a civilian whose fight-or-flight response was heavily weighted toward "freeze." She made a mental note to work on that sometime, but it would have to wait.

Joe pulled the truck in behind the older pickup, effectively blocking it in. If the man with the beard was going to escape, it would be on foot.

Sylvia jumped out of the truck and raced toward the front door. Slipping once or twice, she finally ascended the porch steps with only a minimal amount of snow in her boot. She grabbed the doorknob and twisted and pulled vigorously, but to no avail.

Joe and Eli came up next to her, Joe giving her a scolding look. He growled, "Don't do that again. You're not in charge here."

Sufficiently chastised, she nodded sheepishly but banged on the door anyway.

"Do you mind?" Joe snapped. "You are not law enforcement. Don't make me lock you in the truck."

"Shh," Sylvia demanded. "Did you hear that?"

The trio fell silent and slid closer to the door.

"There it was again. Did you hear it?"

Joe and Eli nodded in unison. "It sounded like a groan," Eli observed.

"Sounds like somebody's hurt," Joe agreed.

"It could be Marian. Get that door open," Sylvia implored.

Eli retrieved a crowbar from the truck, and the two men went to work prying the door open. Sylvia tapped her foot impatiently, attracting disapproving looks from both of them.

With a creak, the wood around the lock splintered and

the door swung open. Without waiting for Joe and Eli, Sylvia rushed through the door and tripped over the prone figure of a man whose head was lying in a pool of blood.

"No beard," Sylvia said. "This isn't the guy."

Joe stepped forward and checked the man's neck for a pulse. "It's faint but it's there. Also seems a little erratic."

"We have to get an ambulance out here," Eli said, pulling his cell phone from the clip on his belt.

As Eli dialed, Sylvia narrowed her eyes and knelt next to the man. "Wait a second. This is the same guy. You can see that he recently had a beard." She raised her eyes to meet Joe's. "What happened to him?"

"No idea, but he doesn't look like he'll be posing a problem." Joe stood and carefully stepped around the man.

Sylvia followed suit but rushed past him when she saw Marian tied to a chair in the living room. Tears squeezed out of her eyes as she stooped and pulled the gag off Marian's mouth. "I have never been so happy to see someone in my whole life!" Sylvia squealed, then wrapped her slender arms around Marian.

"Me neither, dear. Can you please untie me? I need to check on Vito."

Working as quickly as she could, Sylvia untied the ropes and peeled the duct tape from Marian's wrists. Other than a stab of guilt when Marian yelped as she pulled the tape off, Sylvia was elated.

Everyone else would be, too.

Finally unbound, Marian took a few unsteady steps toward the unconscious man and squatted down next to him. Putting her hands on his shoulders, Marian shook him gently. "Vito! Vito, wake up."

She was rewarded with a groan as he moved his head from side to side.

"You're going to be okay," Marian assured him. "We'll get you taken care of."

As the lights from the approaching ambulance reflected off the pure-white snow, and taking in Marian's unkempt appearance, Sylvia thought this might be the happiest Christmas she'd ever known.

Sylvia couldn't wait to hear what happened, but watching the man being wheeled from the house on a stretcher and the worry creasing Marian's forehead, she knew getting the details would have to wait.

CHAPTER SIXTY

JOE SLID A mug of coffee across the table and Marian clutched it tightly with her trembling fingers. After the ambulance had come to take Vito, accompanied by Eli, to the hospital, Marian had ridden with Joe and Sylvia back to the station. It seemed almost surreal to know the events of the past few days were over.

"Whenever you're ready, I need to hear about what happened," Joe gently compelled Marian.

Marian took a long drink of the coffee. Where would she start? It wasn't as clear-cut as it might look to someone on the outside who didn't experience it with her.

"I guess I should start at the beginning, when I went to Henry Feinstein's house after we were done caroling. I never made it to the door. I don't even know if I was out of my car when somebody grabbed me. That's the last thing I remember before waking up in an old barn the next day." Marian took another sip and placed the mug on the table in front of her, her fingers still wrapped around it.

"Tell me about waking up that morning."

Dropping her eyes to the dark liquid still in her mug, Marian recounted the experience of waking up on a pile of hay, covered with threadbare blankets. "I was really confused at first, because I didn't remember how I got there. Vito explained everything he could, but unfortunately, even he didn't know who hired him."

Joe sat up straighter at the mention of Marian's kidnapper. "Speaking of Vito, tell me about him. Do you happen to know his last name?"

Marian shook her head slowly. "I never asked and he didn't volunteer it. As far as telling you about him, I don't know much. He grew up on a farm and his dad never believed he would amount to much, though his mom was a really generous woman and was never one to let a neighbor go hungry. He was married a long time ago and has two kids, but he hasn't seen them since his wife ran off with a big-city lawyer a few years ago. Things sort of spiraled downhill from there. He lost his friends and his job, and he's been strapped for cash ever since."

Joe chuckled softly. "I should have known you'd have gotten the guy's whole life story. So far it sounds like a bad country song."

Marian sighed and said, "I guess it does. Poor guy."

Clearing his throat, Joe continued his questions. "While you were learning everything about this guy, did he happen to mention why he kidnapped you and what he hoped to gain from it?"

After another sip, Marian replied, "Somebody contacted him and paid him to take me. He doesn't know who, and I was never able to find out on my own. He'd been out of work for a while and was desperate for money. He never meant any harm to come to me. I could tell that much. I got him drunk on my hot buttered rum and rummaged through his things while he was passed out. I didn't find anything that would lead anywhere, though."

Joe shot a smile at Marian. "Your hot buttered rum, huh? I guess Fred Rooney wasn't making it up, after all."

Marian answered him with a knowing smile. "I sent Vito to the store with a shopping list. I'd hoped the ingredients would tip someone off."

"It did," Joe confirmed. "Unfortunately, we didn't know who the guy was or where he was staying."

Shrugging, Marian said, "Well, I did the best I could. Vito isn't a bad guy. I enjoyed his company quite a lot, as a matter of fact."

Joe raised a skeptical eyebrow. "Except for when he bound and gagged you, I suppose?"

Marian crossed her arms over her chest. "Vito didn't do that. Actually, he had just unlocked the door and was letting me go free. Before I got outside, I heard a noise behind me and saw him in a pile on the floor. I didn't see anybody, though. I knelt over him to see if he was okay, but then somebody grabbed me from behind and tied that gag over my mouth and tied me to the chair."

"Did you recognize the person?"

She pressed her lips together and shook her head. "I'm afraid not. Whoever it was wore a ski mask that hid their entire face. I didn't recognize the voice either. It was really raspy, almost like they were trying to disguise it. Something about the person seemed familiar, but I really couldn't put my finger on it."

"So Vito was letting you go, then an unknown assailant attacked both of you?" Joe clarified.

"That's exactly what happened." Marian paused and chewed her lower lip. "What's going to happen to Vito? I really don't want him to be in jail."

Joe studied her a moment, compassion filling his normally serious dark eyes. "Ever heard of Stockholm Syndrome?"

"I have," Marian admitted. "That's not what this is, though. He's just a regular guy whose life went down the toilet and he found himself in a desperate situation. I *do not* have Stockholm Syndrome," Marian said firmly and glared at Joe as though she dared him to disagree with her.

"Whatever you say," he mumbled. "I think that's everything I need from you for now. I'll need to follow up with you later if there's anything else we need."

"That would be fine," Marian agreed. "I must say, I'm pretty eager to get home."

"I bet." The two stood and pushed their chairs back under the table. "I know of three ladies in particular that won't give you a moment of peace for a while. Nadine, Holly, and Sylvia have been beside themselves worrying about you."

A smile lit up Marian's face. "It will be so good to see them. And I can't believe I missed my own party the other night."

Joe circled the table and pulled Marian into a bear hug. "It's good to have you back. Now, let's get you home."

Marian held onto Joe's arm as they walked through the slushy parking lot and slid into the passenger side of his Jeep, a rental until he replaced the one he'd wrecked last night. Humming Christmas carols the whole way home, Marian tried to focus on the feeling of peace that being home would bring. Instead, she couldn't shake the thought of Vito lying in a hospital room with who knows what kind of injuries, waiting to be taken into custody.

Fifteen minutes later, Joe pulled into her driveway. Marian gasped at the sight of a large group on her lawn, singing "I'll Be Home for Christmas." Tears stinging the backs of her pale-blue eyes, she sent up a prayer of thanks that her Christmas wish had come true, and that she was home for Christmas.

After several hugs and well-wishes from the carolers, Marian went inside to find that it was set up for a party. It looked just as it had three days ago when she set it up herself. Nadine, Holly, and Sylvia stepped out from the kitchen and gathered her in a group hug.

She wouldn't miss her party after all. Only this time, the winter solstice wasn't the biggest reason to celebrate.

CHAPTER SIXTY-ONE

FRESHLY SHOWERED AND wrapped in her favorite red flannel robe and sipping herbal tea, Marian sat on her sofa with Nadine and Holly, who'd refused to leave her side since she returned home.

"I wonder if there's a news report about you?" Holly said, picking up the remote to the TV and clicking it on.

"I certainly hope not," Marian said, taking another sip of her tea. "I just want to put the whole messy business behind me."

"Oh, come on. You had the whole town worried sick. Everyone loves you." With a mischievous grin, Holly continued, "You're something of a celebrity around here, and even more so now that you were kidnapped."

"What a lovely thing to be known for," Marian said flatly and sank further into her robe, relishing the familiar comfort.

"Look!" Nadine said. "Isn't that where the kidnapper kept you?"

Marian placed her mug on the coffee table and leaned forward. "It certainly is," she confirmed.

"And isn't that the reporter who was covering our Christmas caroling event?" Holly added.

Narrowing her eyes, Marian pursed her lips and said, "It sure is. I wonder what she's doing reporting about this. From what I gathered, she reports fluff stories. You know, things that make you feel good, like dogs rescuing children from burning buildings or dolphins saving swimmers from shark attacks."

Nadine reached over and squeezed Marian's hand. "You being home is certainly something to feel good about."

"I feel good about it, but I can't help but worry about Vito. He truly is a nice guy," Marian said, more to herself than to her companions.

"But Marian—" Nadine began.

"Shhh," Holly commanded. "I want to hear what the reporter has to say."

As they watched Carol Ling's eyes flash with excitement as the old farmhouse served as a somber backdrop, they listened intently as she spoke. *"It's been nearly three days since Marian Bright, one of the town's most beloved citizens, went missing following the first-annual Christmas caroling event celebrating the winter solstice. She disappeared without a trace shortly after the singing concluded, her car abandoned in front of Henry Feinstein's house. Sources say that Mr. Feinstein was a suspect in her disappearance until video footage of an unknown man dragging her away in an old pickup truck was uncovered. Recent developments, however, have cleared Mr. Feinstein of any wrongdoing and Marian has been found and returned home, safe and sound. When the sheriff, Joe Adler, and his deputy, Eli Nolan, arrived at the house behind me, they found Marian bound and gagged and tied to a chair. The man, who is believed to have been her kidnapper, was discovered unconscious on the floor after sustaining a head wound. The sheriff's department has released the man's name, and we now know that the kidnapper was one Vito Franks. What is still unclear is the motive for the crime, and why he specifically targeted Marian Bright. If you have any information, please call the sheriff's department immediately. Make sure you tune in to WGNN, We're the Good News Network, for further developments on this story. This is Carol Ling, wishing you joy and a very Merry Christmas."*

"That was a nice story," Nadine commented.

"It was. And I hope that Vito Franks guy gets what's coming to him," Holly added.

At Marian's silence, the two women looked at her to see her lost in thought, her lips pressed together.

"What is it?" Nadine inquired.

Marian shook her head. "I think I'm remembering something."

Holly arched an eyebrow at the older lady. "What?"

"Never mind. Please hand me the phone."

Doing as Marian requested, Holly exchanged looks with Nadine, who shrugged in return.

Marian dialed quickly and waited a moment for someone to answer her call, then said urgently, "Joe, can you and Eli come over to my house? I know who is behind all this."

CHAPTER SIXTY-TWO

JOE PLACED THE phone back in its cradle and exhaled. "Let's go, Eli. Marian says she knows who was behind her kidnapping and wants us to come right away."

"That was fast. Who is it?"

"She didn't say, but we need to find out before whoever it was realizes she's home and tries again."

Glad that the case might soon be solved, they walked to the temporary vehicle Joe was driving until his own truck was fixed or replaced. Driving in total silence, each man lost in his own thoughts, they arrived at Marian's house fifteen minutes later.

Before they even reached the front steps, the door swung open and Nadine was standing there motioning them inside. After a quick peck on her cheek, Joe walked over to Marian, who was still sitting on the sofa, a dazed look on her face.

"Here we are, Marian. What do you have to tell us?" Joe asked gently, noticing the look of shock on Marian's usually smiling face.

She shifted her gaze to Joe. "I'm pretty sure I know who ordered my kidnapping, but I have no idea why."

Careful not to rush her but wanting desperately to make her tell him, he said gently, "Tell me about it."

To the astonishment of everyone present—Joe, Eli, Nadine, and Holly—Marian laid out her theory and the evidence to back it up.

Joe chewed his lip and looked at Eli, who was nodding toward him. "Makes sense," Eli said. "The 'why' is still a big question, though."

"It sure is. I guess we better go find out," Joe agreed. With that, they stood and walked out into the cold, Christmas Eve air in search of the person who'd ordered Marian to be held hostage just days before Christmas.

CHAPTER SIXTY-THREE

KRIS JINGLE SAT with his parents in their living room, gaping at the TV after Carol had just given the report on Marian's safe return.

"How did she know Henry Feinstein was a suspect?" James Jingle asked, stroking his full, white beard. "From what I understand, Joe has been pretty tight-lipped about the investigation. I can't imagine that he'd go shooting his mouth off to a reporter."

Kris felt his face burning and could only imagine what shade of red it was. A sick feeling began in the pit of his stomach. He knew how Carol had known, because he's the one who told her they suspected Henry to begin with. It had been he who saw Henry Feinstein in the back of the cruiser, and he told her about it.

"Son, are you okay?" James said, concern marring his face.

Managing a slow nod, Kris finally was finally able to form the word "yes" in his mouth, which suddenly was dry.

Just as a concerned mother would, Patricia stood from her

chair and sat next to Kris on the sofa, placing a comforting hand on his forearm. "Kris, what is it?" she urged.

Swallowing over the lump in his throat, he squeaked, "It's me. I'm the source."

"The source? You mean you're the one that gave Carol the information she used in her report?" The disapproval on James's face made Kris want to find a hole to slink into.

Kris nodded. "I saw him in the cruiser with Joe and Eli heading toward the station, but I didn't know she would tell the whole world. At least she didn't mention that I'm the one who told her… at least, not yet."

James shook his head. "You can't trust these people, son. They only care about getting the story, not the people who help them along the way."

Kris stiffened. "That's not fair, Dad. Carol is a very thoughtful person."

Snorting his disagreement, James settled back into his green-and-red-plaid chair and crossed his arms over his barrel chest. "She used you. She used you and was so convincing that she has you believing she actually cares about you."

Of the emotions vying for the primary spot, anger finally won, and Kris leapt from his spot on the sofa. "That's not true!" he shouted. "She wasn't using me. Carol cares about me. I know she does."

A knock at the door stopped the shouting, and Patricia went to answer it while father and son glared at each other. Several seconds later, Patricia re-entered the living room, trailed by WGNN reporter Carol Ling.

"Carol, I just saw your report," Kris said, unable to keep a hint of betrayal out of his voice.

She stepped toward him and grasped his hands in hers. "I can explain."

From his chair, James snorted again.

Patricia cleared her throat and whispered, "James, why don't we give these two some privacy?"

"What for?" he growled. "This is my house."

Shooting him a warning look, Patricia jerked her head toward the kitchen, communicating that James had better follow her, or else...

"Go on," Kris challenged. "Start explaining."

"You know I usually get the fluff pieces, the soft news. Nobody respects or even cares about my stories. I've never gotten the chance to do a real news story before. When this landed in my lap, I thought I could use the things you told me to beef up the story. The sheriff's department certainly wasn't giving me anything." She tilted her head and looked at Kris with pleading eyes. "You aren't mad, are you?"

Kris felt his fury begin to evaporate, and he sighed. "To tell you the truth, I don't know what I feel right now. If you had just asked for help, I would have done anything I could to give you the information you need. Now it just feels like you used me to get information on a story you were doing."

"Kris..." Carol began but didn't continue.

"You have to admit how this looks."

Carol nodded in agreement, her black hair bouncing as her head bobbed. "I do. But nobody knows where I got the information, and nobody is going to know. I won't say a word. I promise." She leaned against his chest and looped her arms around his waist.

Kris stiffened.

The sound of someone banging on the door startled them and Kris pulled away.

Patricia rushed from the kitchen and through the living room. "Don't mind me," she said quickly as she made her way toward the front door. A minute later, Kris's mother, always supportive, stood in the background as Sheriff Adler and Deputy Nolan walked into the living room. The stern look on their faces communicated that someone was in trouble, and Kris had the distinct feeling that someone found out he was the one Carol got the information from.

Kris felt sweat begin to dampen his armpits as he watched Joe pull handcuffs from his belt. Surely giving information to Carol hadn't been so bad a crime that he'd be arrested, though it did seem that ending up in handcuffs was becoming a Christmas tradition for him.

Joe spoke first, taking a step toward Kris and Carol. "Carol Ling, I'm placing you under arrest for kidnapping and assault."

Kris's mouth fell open. "You can't be serious!"

"I'm afraid so," Joe said, then led Carol out of the house, reciting the Miranda warning while the others looked on in shocked horror.

"I knew she was up to no good," James said triumphantly, only to be elbowed in the ribs by Patricia.

Kris sank back onto the couch, his face buried in his hands. "This is the worst Christmas ever!" he wailed, though he had to admit that, deep down, he'd known there was something off about Carol from the beginning.

CHAPTER SIXTY-FOUR

JOE SLID INTO a chair across the table from Carol Ling in the interrogation room at the station. Here was a slender woman, about five feet four inches, with long black hair and almond-shaped eyes that invited him to trust her.

Nobody would ever suspect somebody like her to be the mastermind of a kidnapping plot, he thought as he worked out in his head how he would begin questioning her.

Carol shifted uncomfortably in her seat as she subconsciously picked at her thumbnail. This was certainly not where she'd expect to be on Christmas Eve. Though she wouldn't have been there if she hadn't broken the law.

Clearing his throat, Joe began with the most basic question he could think of to connect her to the kidnapping case. "So, tell me how you ended up reporting on Marian Bright's kidnapping when you were supposed to be in Saddle Hill covering the town's Christmas festivities."

Carol shrugged and stopped picking at her thumbnail. "Luck of the draw, I guess. Since I was already here, I figured, why not? Our station very rarely gets to cover hard-hitting news stories."

"*We're the Good News Network.*"

"Exactly," Carol agreed fervently. "We're never taken seriously, and honestly, I'm shocked that more people don't tune in to watch the stories we cover. The world is full of awful things, and those have plenty of media coverage. The good things that happen and the good people who make a difference every day… those are the stories people *need* to be hearing. Honestly, I think there would be less anxiety and depression in the world if the bad stuff was balanced by the good stuff."

"I agree with you about that," Joe said, then followed it with a challenge. "What I'm having a hard time wrapping my head around is why your station—and you in particular— would be interested in covering a kidnapping. That doesn't sound much like good news. In fact, it sounds like more of the stuff you just said is causing anxiety and depression."

Carol leaned forward and placed her palms on the table. "That's just it. Things could have worked out really bad for Marian. I mean, who knows what that deranged man had planned for her. But instead of harm coming to her, you rescued her. It's a wonderful human-interest story. A well-loved pillar of the community goes missing, only to be rescued from an unknown outcome by local law enforcement. That's the kind of story people truly crave. Dire situations with happy endings." Satisfied that she'd pled her case well, Carol leaned back in her chair and crossed her arms.

Pressing his lips together and nodding, Joe finally said, "I can see that. I know I love happy endings. Almost everyone does. But I'm not so sure this one has a happy ending. In fact, I don't think the end of this story has even been written yet."

A frown crept between Carol's eyebrows. "What do you mean?"

"What I mean is, we don't believe Vito Franks was working alone." Joe leaned forward to close the gap between them. "Tell me, Ms. Ling, how did you know that Marian was gagged and tied to a chair?"

Fear flitted across Carol's face, then disappeared as quickly as it came. "I'm a reporter, Sheriff Adler. It's my job to dig up information about stories."

"Then please, tell me where you got this information."

Carol huffed indignantly. "Surely you know that I won't reveal my sources."

"Assuming there is an actual source," Joe challenged.

Her mouth forming a hard, straight line, Carol spat, "And just what is that supposed to mean?"

"I mean, let's try this out for the ending of the story." Joe leaned back in his chair and interlaced his fingers on the table in front of him. "Vito Franks is a nice guy, but down on his luck, making him ripe for the picking as a fall guy. Let's say somebody knows this about him and decides he would be the perfect person to hire to carry out the plan to kidnap Marian Bright. He's in a financial crisis, so of course he accepts the offer. Unfortunately for the person who hired him, Vito has a soft spot for doing the right thing, and after three days of holding Marian hostage, he decides he wants to let her go."

"Interesting theory, but this is sounding more like fiction than fact," Carol sneered. "Maybe you should consider a career in storytelling."

"Or in the news media," Joe shot back.

Carol glared at him. "Funny, but don't consider being a stand-up comic."

"Oh, that's cute," Joe said, his dislike for this beautiful woman growing with each passing moment. "Let's finish this story. So, good-hearted Vito decides to let Marian go, but the person that hired him shows up just before he can get her out the door. She bonks him on the head and knocks him out, then ties Marian up and gags her."

"We already know that she was tied up and gagged, thanks to my source." Carol smiled triumphantly, clearly under the impression that she'd won.

"Yes, and kudos to you for knowing that. The only problem is, no one knew except us, Marian, and whoever tied her up. Think about how that makes you look."

Carol's eyes flashed and her face flushed red. "What exactly are you accusing me of?"

"Let's see how this ending works for the story." He unlaced his fingers and tapped an index finger on the table. "You got sick of playing second fiddle to your colleagues that report actual news stories. My guess is that they make fun of you because you report the fluffy stories. You know, the kind that make people feel warm and fuzzy about life. Instead of sticking with the stories you're assigned to, you decided to manufacture a story that would earn you a little more credibility as a reporter. How does that sound?"

With a flash of bravado, Carol clapped condescendingly. "Very good, Sheriff. The only problem with that theory is that you have no proof."

Joe smirked. "Except for one thing. We have eyewitness testimony."

Her eyes widening, Carol swallowed hard. "That's ridiculous," she said, her voice coming out in a squeak.

"Afraid so. Marian recognized your movements. We've got you."

Carol's steely resolve had broken. Tears began streaming down her face. "I didn't mean any harm!" she wailed. "I just wanted to make a name for myself. You're right, other reporters do poke fun at me for only reporting things that make the viewer feel good. They say I'm missing out on the most important facts. I just wanted a chance to prove I could do more."

Confession obtained, Joe stood and pushed his chair back, switched off the recorder, and exited the interrogation room. He'd alert Eli that the jail would have another resident, then fill out the necessary paperwork.

He'd done his job. Marian was home, Vito Franks and Carol Ling were now behind bars, and the town could continue with its Christmas celebrations.

Glancing at the clock, Joe noted that there were only a few more hours of Christmas Eve left. He signed his name to the bottom of the paperwork, hummed a few bars of "I'll Be Home for Christmas," then walked out of the station, proud that because of his and Eli's hard work, Marian could say the same thing.

CHAPTER SIXTY-FIVE

Christmas Day

CHRISTMAS BEGAN CLEAR and bright, the snow glistening in the morning sun. Marian had spent hours sitting next to her Christmas tree, drinking coffee with eggnog creamer, thankful that she was home.

Now, she sat surrounded by the people she loved most. The tradition of sharing Christmas dinner together began last year after Ralph's star had been recovered and the thieves arrested. Marian, sitting in the seat of honor this year, glanced from face to face. Her friends were even more like family this year. Nadine, radiant with the expectant glow of motherhood, sat next to Joe, who, for good reason, looked pretty proud of himself.

He should be, Marian mused. I wouldn't be sitting here tonight if it wasn't for him.

Holly sat next to Eli, their hands entwined under the table. Love was in the air, and Marian knew Eli had purchased a ring from Ralph and planned to propose to Holly on New Year's Eve.

Ralph and Carla Stockton, the newlyweds of the group, still beamed at each other. Carla's efforts to find her warmed Marian's soul. Though they hadn't been great friends before, Marian had a feeling that was about to change.

James and Patricia Jingle looked much more comfortable with each other than they had a year ago at this time. James had settled in nicely to being a "civilian," as he preferred to call wearing regular clothes. Marian was proud of the progress he'd made.

The outlier of the group was Kris. Marian didn't think he could look more depressed and dejected than if he'd lost everyone and everything he cared about. In a sense, she guessed he had. News had traveled fast that his girlfriend was the one behind Marian's kidnapping, and it was rumored that Kris felt stupid and embarrassed for being taken in by a pretty face and used to get information about Marian and the kidnapping for her reports. How could he not feel that way? Carol Ling was a cold woman, a pretty face that had sucked in a man who was vulnerable to flattery. Marian unconsciously shook her head. Poor Kris.

As her gaze drifted farther down the table, her joy wavered. There was someone else she wanted to see at the table. Vito hadn't been a bad guy, and he'd treated her well. After only three days together, she considered him a friend.

He should be here, she told herself, feeling guilty that she had something to do with him being in jail. She shook her head. Of course it wasn't her fault. He's the one that made the choice to kidnap her and hold her hostage for three days.

But he'd also made the choice to let her go, and gotten clubbed on the head for his effort.

No, Vito didn't belong in jail. He shouldn't go unpunished, of course, but probation seemed a fair punishment for his crime.

The issue decided, Marian picked up her butter knife and clinked it on the side of her water glass. She cleared her throat and began, "First of all, I want to thank all of you for your efforts in searching for me. If it wasn't for you, I wouldn't be here to enjoy this beautiful celebration of Christmas." Her gaze landed on Sylvia. "And it was lovely to see your wonderful face coming to rescue me."

The room erupted with cheers and happy chatter. Clinking her glass again, Marian continued. "There is one person missing from this table that I have grown quite fond of, and I hope you all would come to see him the way I do." Marian was met with confused stares. "Vito Franks, my kidnapper, is a dear man who fell on hard times. He was injured while he was trying to do the right thing and allow me to escape. He risked his own safety to make that happen." She turned her eyes toward Joe. "My wish is that you would take this suggestion to the judge: that Vito receive probation instead of jail time."

Gasps filled the room at Marian's request. Joe just shook his head.

"Are you sure you want that?" Sylvia asked.

"Positive." Marian turned her eyes back toward Joe. "If you don't go to the judge, I will. He was an old friend of Roger's, and I think he'll listen to me. I'd prefer to go through the proper channels, though. If you won't do it, however, I'll have to go over your head to make sure it happens."

Satisfied with her announcement, Marian resumed eating. She shoveled a bite of mashed potatoes into her mouth and smiled.

As the chatter began again, another clinking sound got the attention of the group. Mayor Becky Roswell, not really a friend but a respected member of the community, stood from her seat at the table. "The town has had a few hard days leading up to today," she said, then looked toward Marian with a sad smile. "The first thing I want to do is apologize for inviting Carol Ling to our town. I thought it would be good publicity, but as we all know, it turned out to be a huge mistake."

"You had no way of knowing the kind of person she really was," Marian said, then cast a glance toward Kris, whose head was bowed in pain and embarrassment. "None of us saw it coming. It's all okay now."

The mayor nodded slightly then cleared her throat. "While there were some truly terrible things going on in Saddle Hill, there were a few people who stood out and rose to the task of making our town even more remarkable. I'd like to recognize those people now." Becky stooped over and pulled a few plaques from the oversized bag sitting next to her chair. "But first, I'd like to announce the winner of our contest to name the Christmas caroling event."

Silence fell over the group gathered around the table as they all exchanged curious glances.

"The winner has been a member of our community their entire life and has brought joy to countless members of this community. In fact, I sat on his lap and told him what I wanted for Christmas when I was a child." A smile broke out on Becky's face. "Without further ado, I'd like to announce that from now on, our Christmas caroling event will be called 'A Hometown Christmas,' named by our very own resident Santa, James Jingle."

Cheers erupted from the table, and several people slapped James on the back with congratulations.

"As promised, you will be receiving a platter of baked goods from the Rose Petal Café, baked by our very own Nadine Adler," the mayor reminded.

James beamed at the news that he'd been chosen as the winner of the contest, while the mayor clinked her glass again to regain the group's attention.

"I have two awards to hand out for citizens that have gone above and beyond this Christmas to ensure that Saddle Hill remains the kind of place we all love." Becky looked around the table and smiled at each person present. "The first award is our 'Service Award.' For going to great lengths in order to bring Marian home, and even crashing his vehicle, Joe Adler has been a wonderful sheriff this year, and his bravery in the face of this crisis has shown that the townspeople made the right decision in electing you."

Nadine beamed at her husband, pride written on her face, as everyone else offered their congratulations.

Gaining control of the crowd again, Mayor Becky Roswell continued. "The second award is our 'Outstanding Citizen' award. This person surprised me by going out of their way to make sure the less fortunate had what they needed for Christmas. Kris Jingle, you went above and beyond the call of your duty as Santa by personally fulfilling a little boy's Christmas wish list. Because of you—with some help from Nadine—a family is eating heartily tonight, and the homeless of Saddle Hill have the personal care items they need."

Marian could see that Kris's eyes were red with unshed tears, and he was struggling to keep his emotions in check. It had been a rollercoaster for him. Her heart swelled at the good people that surrounded her. An unlikely hero and one that did heroic things in the name of the job were recognized by everyone for the good things they'd done to help others.

Marian smiled. This was a good night, made even better by her Christmas wish having come true.

She was home for Christmas.

EPILOGUE

January 1st

NEW YEAR'S DAY held promises for a bright future. Accompanied by a newly engaged Eli Nolan, Marian and Vito stepped out of Eli's truck and walked up the steps onto the porch of the old farmhouse.

"What are we doing here? If it's all the same to you, I'd like to leave this part of my life behind and never think about this place again," Vito remarked as Marian stuck the key that Vito had once worn around his neck into the lock.

"What if I told you it was going to be a while before you could get this place out of your mind?" Marian said, a twinkle in her eye and a mischievous grin on her face.

Vito looked between Marian and Eli. "What's going on? Did you bring me here to torture me? Maybe lock me up in a closet or stick me out in the barn?"

"Don't be nervous," Eli said. "Marian has this all figured out."

She twisted the key in the lock and pushed the front

door open. "So, I'm thinking we need to restore the floors throughout, maybe take that wall down so the entryway opens more into the living room, and paint the walls a nice, calming color." Marian continued walking forward into the main living area. "I'd also like to resurface the fireplace, possibly hang a very special clock made of a tiller blade over there, and get all new furnishings."

Vito cast a confused look toward Marian. "What are you talking about?"

Ignoring his question, Marian continued on to the kitchen. "This will need a complete gut job to make it functional for our purposes, but I'd like to retain the character if possible."

"What are 'our purposes'?" Vito asked to no response.

They continued throughout the house, Marian making comments about improvements she'd like to make to each of the rooms.

"Will somebody please tell me what this is all about?" Vito demanded impatiently when they came back to the living room.

Eli and Marian exchanged a conspiratorial glance. "Well," Marian began, "I haven't been able to get this old house out of my head. And not just because I was held here against my will. Though I should be thoroughly traumatized, I fell in love with it sometime during the three days I was here, so I bought it."

Vito's mouth gaped open. "You *bought* it? Why?"

Marian smiled at his surprise. "When I was rummaging through the junk in here, I found that this place used to be a bed-and-breakfast. It was called the Farmhouse Inn. I found out who owned it and made an offer. I plan to restore it and reopen it as a bed-and-breakfast." She looked at Eli who gave her an encouraging nod. "You're on probation," she said to

Vito, "and part of the terms of your probation are to get a job. For the foreseeable future, your job is to help me restore this house." She waved her hands around the room.

"You can't be serious," he challenged. "I mean, I'm grateful that you went to bat for me to get me out of jail and onto probation, but this place doesn't have great memories. I don't like the person I was when I was here."

Marian shrugged. "So then I guess it's time to rewrite those memories. You get to change this place from the dilapidated house that was once used to keep a kidnapping victim, to a place where others will come for rest, relaxation, and to reconnect with each other. That's quite a noble calling, I'd say. Plus, won't that be quite an entertaining story for the guests?"

"I don't know…" Vito protested.

She reached for his arm and gave it a squeeze. "Remember Roger's words. 'Grow where you're planted.' Right now, you're planted here. With us working together, we're going to make this place spectacular. The guests will flock to it."

Vito nodded slightly and turned around, taking in the spaces in view. "You know, while we were here, I kept thinking about how I'd redo this place if given the chance. I guess this is my chance."

Marian smiled at him and sighed. "It's *our* chance. Our chance to turn painful memories into something beautiful."

Acknowledgements

Once again, many thanks are in order for the creation of this book. To my editor, Dierdre Stoelzle, who provided a keen eye for detail and encouraging comments while suggesting ways to make the story better.

Robynne, at Damonza, for creating a beautiful book, inside and out.

To my husband, Billy, and daughters, Zoe and Nora, as well as many friends and family who have encouraged me through this process. You have no idea how much your support means to me!

Finally, to you, the reader. Thank you for taking a chance on me and picking up this book. I hope you have enjoyed reading this story as much as I enjoyed writing it.

Until next time!

Erin

www.ingramcontent.com/pod-product-compliance
Lightning Source LLC
Chambersburg PA
CBHW021128190726
48288CB00008B/2557